Edie's Books

ROMANTIC SUSPENSE

Truth About Love & Murder, book 1
Rules of Love & Murder, book 2
A Love & Murder Christmas, book 3
Raining Love & Murder *coming soon!*

CONTEMPORARY ROMANCE

Rescued Hearts series
Hearts in Motion, book 1
Christmas at Angel Lake, book 2
Crazy Sexy Love, book 3
Finding Awesome, book 4

Miracle Interrupted series
Must Worship Cats, book 1 (a novella)
Stardust Miracle, book 2
Miracle Lane, book 3
Miracle Pie, book 4
Mo's Heart, book 5

A Love & Murder Christmas

Love & Murder, Book 3

Edie Ramer

Published by Blue Walrus Books

ISBN: 978-1-939328-27-4

Cover design by EJR Digital Art
Copy-editing by Blue Otter Editing
Proofreading by Judicious Designs
Formatting by Author E.M.S.

Published in the United States of America.

One

I wish these assignments came with instructions. ~Pooka

"Have you heard from Paul?" Lauren Finney's precise tone of voice made Darryl Morton grip the phone tightly.

Beads of sweat popped out on Darryl's neck and face and inside the folds of fat. It was the first Monday of October, and Lauren had called the Finney Insurance Agency every first Monday since Paul Finney had gone missing, more than four and a half years ago.

Darryl hated first Mondays.

"No, I haven't. I'm sorry." He always said, *I'm sorry.* He was sorry, all right. Sorry about this whole damn thing.

"Have you heard anything about him?" she asked, and there was something new in her voice. Weariness. Defeat.

"I'm sorry. I haven't heard anything." Now his hand holding the phone was sweaty, too.

"Nothing has changed," she said. "Nothing."

He looked around the front office of the agency. He could tell her that his chair was getting smaller every day, and he needed a larger one. Or that a lawyer had moved next to their agency's office in the strip mall on the edge of the city.

But that wasn't what she meant.

There was a silence, and he swallowed again. Silence was new, too. Silence was an enemy. It meant she was thinking.

Then she thanked him and said good-bye, her tone normal again.

But it was too late for normal. Normal had passed them by when Paul had disappeared.

And then there was a new normal. A normal that Darryl had created out of necessity and desperation.

The next new normal would not bode well for him. Not after what he'd been doing since Paul's disappearance.

He needed to think of alternative solutions.

He jerked open his drawer, reached into it, pulled out a chocolate bar, ripped off the paper, stuffed the whole bar into his mouth, and chewed as fast as he could.

Some days he thought that going to prison would be a relief. Then he would picture the people who counted on him.

He couldn't go to prison. He just could not.

Two

I smell trouble.
~Pooka

Three weeks later

One step into her bedroom, Tori Donahue froze, staring at a black cat that was curled up on her fluffy, oval area rug.

A *big* black cat. *Giant*-sized.

Her breath whooshed out. She was shaking, her heart beating fast, and she didn't know if it was from fear or excitement. Hard to tell with the oversized cat curled up, but it might be as tall as she was. Five two and still growing.

And what made it freakier—as if a giant cat napping in her room wasn't freaky enough—she and her dad didn't have a cat. Not even a regular-sized one.

One thing for sure, it didn't come from her imagination. In all her twelve years, she'd never imagined a giant cat sleeping in her bedroom.

Who would? She'd imagined her favorite boy band. All four of them, with their cute hair—especially the cute one with the puffy lips—telling her that she should sing with them, and they'd teach her how to play the guitar because they loved her smile and the way she danced.

But not anything near this. Things like this didn't happen in Trouble Bay, Wisconsin. A tiny town in Door County, in the middle of a long slice of land with Lake Michigan surrounding it on three sides. Which meant miles of water and, for almost half of the year, a flood of tourists. The other half was like living in the middle of a snowy playground. Just school and winter sports—if you liked that kind of thing. Otherwise, it was just boring.

Right now, staring at the giant cat in her bedroom, boring sounded good to her.

Maybe this hallucination was a new symptom of her diabetes, though in all the literature, the information from the doctors and the nutritionists, and even the online diabetes group she belonged to, no one had ever said anything about seeing things that weren't there.

Maybe she wasn't really standing here.

Maybe she'd fallen into a coma.

Or maybe she was just sleeping. Maybe this was a freakish dream.

It wouldn't be the first time. And she'd always wanted a cat. Or a dog. Or a horse. When she was younger, she'd begged her dad and mom for a pet. They both were working, and they'd kept saying they weren't home enough to take care of a pet.

Then she was diagnosed, and her parents had

enough trouble taking care of her and worrying about her.

And now there was just Tori and her dad.

She closed her eyes tighter, her face scrunched, listening to the huffs of her exhales then inhales, sucking her breaths deep into her lungs. Over and over, until she felt light-headed and opened her eyes.

Looking at the rug, she blinked.

The cat was still there, still curled up, as if she owned the rug.

Even though Tori saw the cat, she knew it wasn't possible—unless the government had been doing experiments on cats and this one had escaped and had picked Tori to save it.

That would be a cool explanation, and Grandma said not to trust anyone in the government. But her dad would say that it wasn't likely, and he would probably tell her a reason the cat was in the house. Or else say she was just seeing things that weren't there.

Maybe he was right, though it sure looked real.

She closed her eyes again. Tighter this time, holding her lids closed for long seconds. Holding her breath, too, until she felt dizzy.

When she opened her eyes this time, she was swaying in her pink, purple, and yellow running shoes. The cat still lay there, but its head was up now, its eyes open. Blue. Ice blue. They seemed to glow, but Tori had learned in fifth grade that cats had mirror-like cells in the backs of their eyes that reflected light.

That was a year ago, and she'd never forgotten it, even though she'd forgotten most of the math she'd learned and had to learn all over again this year.

As if she'd known that someday there would be a giant, blue-eyed cat in her bedroom.

"Are you real?" she whispered.

The cat didn't say anything, but it didn't go away, either.

She dropped her backpack on her bed with the turquoise quilted bedspread and the purple stripe through the middle that clashed with the red-and-white-striped sheets and pillowcases underneath. She liked things that didn't match. After all, *she* didn't match. Not since she was seven, and the doctors had diagnosed her with diabetes while her mom cried and her dad blinked a lot as his jaw hardened.

He was a former Marine, and her mom said Marines were brave.

Her mom was gone now. A stupid car accident with a stupid, drunken tourist when she was nine. But her dad was still brave.

So was she. Most of the time. But now her hands shook and her heart pounded.

"Are you real?" she asked again.

The cat just watched, not answering her. It reminded her of Josh, the fourteen-year-old boy who lived next door. Sometimes he just looked at her, not saying anything, and she couldn't tell what he was thinking.

Like she did with Josh, she jutted out her chin and moved away from the cat. Heading toward the desk in the corner, though she wouldn't do *this* with Josh watching her.

Feeling the eyes of the cat on her, she got out

her kit in a makeup bag. Putting her testing stuff in the bag didn't fool anyone at school, but it made her feel more normal. In a small town like Trouble Bay, everyone knew everyone else's business.

That's what almost everyone liked to say. Except Grandma. Grandma was pretty sure that *everyone* was wrong, and that some people kept their business to themselves. Especially their naughty business.

Tori wished they'd keep out of her business. She couldn't even have a cold without people wondering if she was dying.

Grandma liked to say that people were just plain stupid.

Tori was pretty sure that Grandma was right. Even the smartest people did dumb things. And no one should get Tori started on the teachers. Some were nice, but others could give the wicked witches in Oz lessons on torturing kids.

Tori had washed her hands downstairs already, so it only took a minute to insert a test strip into the meter, poke her fingertip, then hold the test strip over the globule of blood that bubbled out. The numbers on the meter were good, so she threw her test strip in the wastebasket below the desk, then put everything away and zipped up the bag. Ready to use again after eating.

When she turned to the cat, it was standing.

A chill went through Tori, but it was a delicious chill.

"Yesss," the cat said.

Tori stared at the cat, her jaw dropped.

The cat stared back, its jaw just fine.

"Did you really talk?" Tori asked. "Or did I imagine it?"

"Yessss," the cat said.

It talked! It really talked! "Yes, what?"

"Yesss, I'm real. Yesss, I talk."

"Ooooh." Tori's heart was beating like a hammer hitting a long row of nails, one at a time, really fast. "Can I touch you?"

The cat stretched its head toward her. Tori lifted her hand toward the long neck, her breath stuck in her throat, afraid to scare the giant cat away.

As soon as her fingertips grazed the softest fur she'd ever touched, the cat purred.

Joy sparked inside Tori. She could feel it in her chest, like little starbursts. Maybe she was dreaming, because this couldn't really be happening.

Or else she was hallucinating.

Her hand stilled on the soft fur, and she exhaled and inhaled again.

"Most likely," she said out loud, "I'm in a coma. I'm dying."

Three

Let the human games begin.
~Pooka

In the upper hallway, passing his daughter's bedroom with the door cracked open an inch, Adam Donahue overheard her words, each one an ice pick in his chest.

He whipped around and rushed into her room. "Tori!"

Blinking, she swiveled to look at him. Too thin, too frail, too pale.

But she was standing.

She was alive.

His heart still thundered too loud and too fast, but he sucked in a breath and let it slowly out while she stared at him as if there were horns growing out of his head.

He wouldn't be surprised. In fact, he wouldn't be surprised if weeds sprouted out of his head.

If they did, he wanted them to be marijuana. Some nights he could use a little help, though so far he'd stuck to the occasional beer. He had to be alert for Tori. Just in case she needed him.

"You are not dying." He enunciated the words clearly.

She looked over her shoulder and frowned, then back to him. "You don't see it?"

"See what?"

"Anything else in the bedroom?"

He stepped inside to look around, but all he saw was her bed with the bright girly colors and her dresser and desk and double windows that let the sun shine in. A room that made her happy. And if it made her happy, it made him happy.

As happy as he could be after three years of silently grieving.

"A bug?" He squinted and peered around again. Nothing. Kneeling, he leaned forward and looked under the bed, not spotting anything there, either. "A mouse?"

She sighed. The dad is useless sigh that reminded him she was going to be a teenager in January, though she'd perfected that sigh at least a year ago. "Never mind."

"What is it? What's going on?" He stood. He wasn't letting her get away with the never minds. Even when he wanted to. After Noelle's funeral, his wife's best friend, Lauren, had forced him to be proactive with Tori. Since then, whenever he felt like sitting in a chair to mindlessly watch TV all night, letting Tori do her own thing, he could hear Lauren's voice in his head. "You want to lose her, too? If you don't force her to talk to you, that's what will happen. Even if she acts like she doesn't want to talk to you, talk to her anyway. Otherwise the walls will thicken, and you won't be able to bust through them."

Tori looked away from him, toward the window. "Okay," she said, but she didn't seem to be talking to him.

He frowned. What was going on?

She turned back to him. "You're not going to believe me."

"If you tell me you're telling the truth, then I believe you."

"It is the truth." There was a resigned look on her face. Like she'd had after Noelle's fatal accident. Not right away, but later. Nothing like the fear and confusion on her face when she'd been diagnosed. She'd been younger then. Seven. Things like that weren't supposed to happen to kids. And they really weren't supposed to happen to her.

The diagnosis had pretty much prepared her for rotten things happening, no matter how much he'd tried to shield her. And it wasn't as if he could shield her from her mother's death.

"Tell me." He braced himself, because he was ready for rotten things happening, too.

"There's a giant cat in the room that only I can see." Her voice was flat. Defeated.

Fear razored up Adam's spine.

"She talks," Tori continued, "but she says only I can hear her."

He looked again in the direction her head had been turned, but still saw nothing. Of course he saw nothing. A giant cat? He'd seen some big cats, though not in his house. When he'd married Noelle, his yellow Labrador retriever had been seventeen. Old for a dog. In the last months of

Ryder's life, Adam had lifted him to take him in and out of the house when he thought that Ryder needed to do his business. And that last, sad week, he'd slept on the floor with Ryder. Not ready to let him go.

Noelle had ended up sleeping on the floor, too, one night, on Ryder's other side. That next morning, he and Noelle had woken up. But Ryder hadn't.

Even now, the memories hurt like a knife buried deep and twisting in his heart.

He'd sworn he would never have another pet. You loved them, and then they died.

A lot like people.

His best buddy from the Marines. And then his wife.

He was not letting go of Tori. No way.

Because he didn't know what else to do, he sucked in a deep breath, then asked, "What's the cat's name?"

The stiffness eased out of her shoulders. The relief on her face squeezed his chest. He'd said the right thing.

"I didn't ask but—" Her mouth open, she looked sideways. Her eyes wide, she nodded, then snapped back to him. "Pooka. The cat said she's a pooka, and we should just call her Pooka."

"Is she here for a reason?"

Tori's head tilted slightly, and once again she turned back to the invisible cat. After a few seconds, she nodded, then shifted back to him.

"She said she's going to help me." She frowned. "She's not telling me more. I don't know what she can do."

"Neither do I."

"You think I'm crazy, Dad?" Her voice was small and her mouth trembled.

If he hadn't been watching her closely, he would've missed it.

"I don't know about crazy," he said. "I only know I love you. That's all that matters."

Tears spurted in her eyes. He stepped up and hugged her. Maybe she was three months away from thirteen, but she would always be his baby girl. He released her and looked down. "You okay?"

She nodded, and he ruffled her hair. "You're the best daughter ever."

"You're the best dad. Except for one thing."

Only one? He could think of a few hundred. "What's that?"

"You can't really see the cat, can you?"

"Honey, I never said I was perfect."

She giggled.

"You'll tell me if the cat tells you anything else?" he asked.

"Maybe. If I think it will bore you, then I won't tell you."

He felt a pinch of fear. She was bargaining with him. Like a teenager. He wasn't ready for her teenage years. He didn't know if he'd ever be ready for that.

"No." He spoke firmly, making sure his voice left no new options. "I want you to tell me everything."

"Dad." She rolled her eyes. "You're going to be really, really bored."

"Love you, sweetheart." He bent and kissed the top of her forehead, just a peck.

She beamed. "Love you, too."

He nodded at the bed. "'Bye for now, Pooka."

Tori giggled again. "Pooka says good-bye to you, too. I think she likes you."

He walked backward. He knew what a pooka was. A fantasy creature. And in this case, a fantasy creature he had to pretend to believe in. "That's because she's a girl, and all the girls love me."

Tori laughed harder, and he grinned at her, but as soon as he turned around, his smile straightened to a line.

He knew what he should do. Call Lauren. They hadn't spoken in more than three years. Since a month after Noelle's funeral, when she'd stopped by to see how he was doing and had given him the advice that had saved his relationship with Tori. Lauren lived two towns over. Only a twenty-minute drive, but he hadn't kept in touch.

To be truthful, after she'd given him the advice, he'd cut her off. He'd always liked Lauren, and she had been right about him talking to Tori. She was usually right, a trait that could be annoying. Or amusing. But his grief had been so strong at the time, and he'd been feeling so lost, he'd been afraid he'd lean too much on her.

Because of that, he'd kept her away from his daughter. He knew it was wrong, but Lauren had her own problems, with no news yet about her husband, who'd disappeared about a year and a half before Noelle's funeral.

Reluctance dragged his footsteps down. He reminded himself that he was stronger now. And this wasn't about him. It was for Tori. It was time to reach out for help.

Not to his parents. They were in the middle of their own family problems. His dad's parents weren't doing well. They lived in the Upper Peninsula in Michigan, and since his dad had retired from the brewery and his mom could sell her home-knit sweaters online from anyplace in the world, his parents were spending more time in the UP than at home.

He didn't expect any support from Noelle's parents, either. They'd left for California two months after Noelle's funeral to be near Noelle's brother and his family.

The only backup they had was Lauren, and this pooka thing scared him. Maybe this wasn't an emergency. Maybe he was panicking. Maybe it would go away.

He wasn't afraid of a lot of things...except when it came to Tori. When she needed help, he wasn't waiting.

Once again, he needed Lauren's help.

Four

The best part of humans is their imagination. But only when they imagine the best. ~Pooka

Lauren rang the bell of the two-story house in the smallish subdivision of medium-sized homes about a mile from the bay. Stepping back, she dropped her hand onto the neck of the tall and dignified Irish wolfhound at her side. The love of her life, she'd often thought.

Falco grounded her. And she needed grounding today. This wasn't how she had planned to spend her Saturday morning, but when Adam Donahue had called her last night, she hadn't been able to turn down his plea for help.

The door opened, and she stared into Adam's blue eyes. Her heart twitched. Her breath sucked in. Her body heated.

The same chemical reactions she'd felt when she was seventeen and her best friend had introduced Lauren to her new boyfriend. A good-looking boy with an unexpectedly low voice—a country-singing man's voice—had smiled at her, not even glancing down her stick-like figure, then dismissing her, the way most guys did.

Though her heart had beat faster, she had narrowed her eyes and told him she'd hoped he was good enough for Noelle. He'd laughed and slung his arm around her shoulders and said he would do his best.

She'd wanted to melt into a hormonal puddle.

She hadn't, of course. Skin and bones didn't melt because of an unwanted sexual attraction. Even at seventeen, she was practical enough to know that. Instead, she'd clung to her common sense and willpower.

And here it was, eighteen years later, and she still looked at him and wanted to melt.

Once again, she overcame it, annoyed by her body's reaction. No wonder she hadn't insisted on stopping by after he'd told her that he and Tori needed to learn how to function without her help. Except for feeling bad about Tori, she'd been *glad* he'd said that. Pretending to be unaffected by him was exhausting.

"So what's this thing about my beautiful, perfect goddaughter?" she asked, making her tone brisk.

He laughed but there was no humor in it. His blue gaze lowered to Falco. "Come in. Both of you. Tori's at a friend's house now and probably won't be back until dinner."

Lauren made a face. "Tori's that age already?"

"She reached that age two years ago. Almost a teenager and she knows everything." He backed up and she and Falco stepped in.

Once in, she looked behind him. As if still

expecting Noelle to dance in and hug her, then say in her laughing voice, *It's about time you came. What took you?*

In her mind, she replied, *My giant crush on your husband.*

Stupid. And she tried to avoid stupid things, though doing stupid things was part of the human condition, like tail wags were part of the canine condition and hair balls were part of being feline. Putting her hand on Falco's neck again, she looked down on him, and he looked up at her. She immediately relaxed.

Everyone should be lucky enough to have a Falco in their life.

"Falco's a great dog," he said, as if reading her thoughts.

"The best." She looked up slightly. At five nine, she was about four inches shorter than Adam. Close enough to see clearly the jawline stubble of his golden-brown hair.

He was a man's man. The kind she'd never dated. She'd always attracted the business type. Men like Paul, who'd wanted a brainy woman with strong opinions at his side.

At least, that's what he'd told her when he'd proposed, and she'd believed him.

Which proved that even smart woman could do stupid things. Especially when the smart woman was harboring a burning desire to have children, and, on paper, this man had seemed the right choice.

Never trust paper. Trust your heart.

She glanced around, her mouth dropping open. *Noelle.* No, it couldn't be.

Oddly, the sentence had ended with a purr.

"Something wrong?" Adam asked.

"My imagination is going crazy."

"Crazy happens sometimes." He held out his hand. "I'll take your coat."

She peeled off her charcoal-gray, insulated trench coat that she deemed practical, stylish, and, most important for Door County residents, warm. As he hung it in the large coat closet off to the side, she stepped into the open floor plan that swept from the kitchen to the dining room and the living area. The walls were a creamy yellow, the couch a rich coral, and the two recliners the color of a milk chocolate bar.

It was all Noelle. Nothing had been changed. No wonder she had imagined hearing Noelle's voice.

Lauren swallowed a lump in her throat, but that didn't soothe the ache in her heart. She missed her laughing friend.

Steps sounded behind her on the wooden floor. Adam. She turned, wanting to smile but not able to dredge one up. Neither did he.

"Coffee?" he asked.

She nodded. Coffee and dark chocolate were her only vices. He led the way to the kitchen, where he poured coffee into two cups. He handed one to her. "Still black and bitter?"

"Black and tasteful," she said.

Laughter sparked in his eyes, though he just grinned, and she grinned back at him. Two old friends. Nothing more.

"Are you ready to talk?" she asked.

"Are you ready to sit down?"

She raised her eyebrows. "So it's going to be a sit-down talk."

"'Fraid so," he said, but he didn't look afraid. He just looked sad, his grin gone along with the sparkle in his eyes.

Sadness seeped into her, too. She glanced at the tall stools at the extended kitchen counter and then turned toward the table. The tabletop was a thick plank that used to be a church door that Adam had reclaimed, and he'd used the legs from an old sewing machine to hold it up.

He'd gotten these items while renovating homes during the winter. Noelle had loved the table. She'd been so proud of Adam. And there was a window on the left with the sunlight pouring in. Though the yards weren't big, bushes gave the house a semblance of privacy.

Lauren took a seat near the end. Holding the coffee mug, she looked outside, and she could almost believe she saw the ghost of her beautiful friend, waving at her.

"You okay?" Adam sat across the table from her.

She lifted the coffee to her mouth and took a large gulp. Setting the mug on the table, she said, "I'm fine. Coffee is the cure." She gazed into his blue eyes. "So, what is it?"

He sat across from her, his big hands cupped around a Disney princess mug. "You're not going to believe it."

"Try me."

"You've always been cynical. What do you know about pookas?"

"Huh?"

"That's what I thought." His forehead furrowed. "Pookas are spirits that come into a house in a large animal form."

She leaned over the table. "Are you okay?"

"I have to be okay for Tori's sake. I overheard her talking in her bedroom. I went in and no one was there. She insisted there was a big cat in the room. A pooka. As big as she is. She was talking to it, and it talked back to her, though I couldn't hear it." He held up his hand to stop her from saying anything. "I know it sounds crazy, but she wasn't kidding me or scamming me. She believed it." He glared at her, as if daring her to doubt him.

"Go on," she said.

"I looked it up online. That's how I found out more about pookas. She said that the cat spoke to her." He shook his head. "She's not lying. And she's not crazy."

Lauren took a deep breath. "If you say she's not lying, I believe you."

"And the crazy part?"

"Not crazy." Two vertical lines formed between her eyebrows. "She does have a good imagination."

A breath huffed out of him. "That's some imagination. If she'd said a dog or a horse, I'd go with that. She's always wanted a dog, and when she was a kid, she was horse crazy. She's never asked for a cat. Not once. If I brought home a kitten, sure, she'd probably love it. But only because it's there."

"So that leaves two things. She's imagining a pooka in her bedroom. Or there really is a pooka in her bedroom." She frowned. "She's twelve. At this age, girls aren't thinking about fictional creatures. They're thinking about boys,"

He groaned, sounding like a rusty door.

"I'm sorry," she said, holding back a hiccuping laugh. "Not that I believe Tori's thinking about boys, but some girls do."

He closed his eyes shut, his mouth clenching, and she winced.

"Back to the cat," she said. "What did it say?"

His eyes opened, and he stared at her. "You're really asking that?"

She shrugged. "That's why you called me, right? Even if there's no cat, no creature, and it's all in her mind, the dialogue she heard—real or imagined—must be important."

"Only you would think that. So you think the pooka is possible?"

Her mouth opened...and then shut. No, of course she didn't think it was possible. She believed in what she could see and what she could touch.

But something stopped her from saying it. "Tori's always been creative."

"She takes after her mom that way. Noelle was the family artist."

Lauren laughed, the ache back in her chest and tears not far away. "Noelle used to say that *you* were the artist." She tapped her knuckles on the table. "Like this. She loved this table that you made. She was always proud of you."

His eyes remained sad. "So what do you think I should do?"

She took another large gulp of her coffee, then

pushed back the chair and stood. Behind her, she could hear the scrape of dog nails as Falco pushed up to his four feet. "I think we should say hi to the pooka. See if it says hi back."

"Tori said it only talks to her."

"But you said it's a cat, right?" She stooped to hug Falco's shoulders, and Falco pressed his head against the side of hers. Then she looked up at the tall, handsome man staring down at them. "Pooka or no, a cat is a cat, and if there's really an invisible cat up there"—she frowned, because this would undoubtedly have a bad ending— "Falco will sniff it out."

Seconds later, as she headed up the stairs, she heard a rhyme in her head: *Fee fi fo fat, I smell the blood of a very big cat.*

Five

I smell dog stink.
~Pooka

Adam let her go ahead of him, the dog behind her. He hung back just far enough to tilt his head to see around the dog and admire Lauren's long legs. Even covered by black jeans, they looked spectacular. The day Noelle had introduced them, Lauren had been wearing shorts. He'd had to force himself not to stare at her legs.

She reminded him of an upscale runway model with her height and her slenderness and the way she stood with her spine so straight under her blue sweater. He liked her face, too. Back then and now. She wasn't beautiful, but she was striking with her sharp cheekbones and triangular, catlike jawline.

Then there was the way she spoke, with perfect pronunciation, as if she were reading out of a textbook. Listening to her amused him, though he hadn't been in a laughing mood for the last three years.

She reached the upstairs hallway and turned into the hall, passing the linen closet and the bathroom. Tori's bedroom door was open—as was his down the hall. She stopped in front of Tori's and looked at him.

That was like her, waiting for permission. Polite, but never in a servile way. Polite in a *what are you waiting for* way. Even her big dog stood solidly at Lauren's side, his head higher than her waist, not showing any impatience. Adam knew men and women with less manners than Falco.

"Go on," he said.

She stepped in, the dog after her. Adam followed the dog again. Low man in the pecking order.

The thought made him want to grin, but he didn't. The only smiles he gave out these days were conscious ones. And now that he wanted to, the act of forming a spontaneous smile seemed to have slipped out of his muscle memory. It was something he needed to relearn.

Like making love.

He'd almost had sex with a woman a year and a half ago. He'd thought it was time, but he'd stopped before it went too far. It had felt wrong.

He'd felt unfaithful.

A low growl stopped his thoughts. He blinked. Standing in the doorway. Lost in his thoughts.

Pulling himself into the here and now, he strode into the room and stopped at Lauren's side. Falco was standing still, his legs stiff, staring at Tori's fluffy rug. A rumble rolled out of his throat.

When Adam had been in the Marines in

Afghanistan, he'd once seen a service dog stand with his legs stiff as he growled at an IED.

It had scared the shit out of him.

"What's wrong with your dog?"

Lauren turned to him, her brown eyes wide, her expression solemn. "This is going to be difficult to process. It's difficult for me, too." She stopped and swallowed. "I believe," she continued, her voice pitched higher than normal, "that Falco sees or senses *something*. I don't know if it's a big cat or a pooka, but it's there and it's real."

"You can't be serious."

The dog growled again, louder, his legs and posture rigid, the shaggy gray hairs raised slightly on his spine.

Lauren motioned at the dog. "Falco's not a jumpy dog. He's normally very calm. Something is obviously there. You can't deny his reaction."

He shook his head. He wanted to deny it, but it was like denying that the sun was shining in the sky outside.

"Don't worry." Her voice softened as she gazed down at the rug. "Falco won't hurt you. Is there anything you want to say to us?"

His breath sucked in, and he held it. As if whatever it was would speak to them.

She waited a moment in silence, then stood straight, her head still angled downward.

He exhaled finally but remained slightly behind her. Was the pooka talking to her? He shook his head. It was insane to even consider it.

At the same time, he *wanted* it to be true, as crazy as the idea was. It would mean his daughter was all right. That she wasn't seeing and hearing things.

If Falco saw it, too...

Something switched inside him. Life was all about believing.

Or about not believing.

Everyone had choices, and right now, he was making his. A choice to believe the unbelievable.

He breathed easier, his hands uncurling. The relief was a light burning brightly inside him, and he wanted to bend down and kiss the dog's shaggy forehead.

As odd and as hard as it was to believe that there was a pooka in his house, Falco had clearly sensed *something*. And he was relieved. As much as he didn't want weird things happening in his house, he wanted less a daughter who was talking to imaginary creatures.

"Are you okay?" Lauren was watching him now with her eyes open wide.

He couldn't speak. Too choked up with relief and emotion. Not just for this moment, but relief for the last three years. Relief for his slow healing. And maybe healing from before that. The eight years he'd been in the Marines, where he'd seen men doing bad things to others out of hatred and anger that had shocked him and angered him and saddened him. That had ripped away his faith in humanity.

He'd returned home to this place that seemed like a paradise compared to where he'd been.

And he'd had Noelle and Tori.

He'd been a lucky man.

And then there'd been Tori's diagnosis.

Then two years later, the accident. The heartbreaking news. And as much as he'd wanted to yell and cry and break things and swear at God and the world, he'd had to be strong for Tori.

Somewhere inside him, he'd shut down a lot of emotions. It had been the only way he could cope.

And now there seemed to be another emotion he couldn't express.

Because either his daughter and Falco were nuts and he was sane...

Or he believed they were sane, which made him nuts.

Nothing was real. Nothing. Nothing but his choices. And nothing but Lauren, because she would never be a fanciful person. If she said her dog saw something, then her dog did see something.

So he reached for her, because maybe *he* was the fanciful person. Maybe something had snapped in his mind. Maybe this whole thing was a figment of his imagination. Maybe she wasn't really here. Maybe nothing was real.

But she felt real under his hands. Her arm in a soft blue sweater beneath his right hand, and her slender back beneath his left. He tugged her closer, to his chest. Her eyes opened wider, and he bent, his eyes closing, and his open mouth locked onto her open mouth. And he kissed her and kissed her and kissed her. He never wanted to stop, and she wasn't trying to stop him. He tugged her closer, and it felt good, so good. He bent his knees slightly, their pelvises lined up, their bodies fitting perfectly. He pressed against her—pressing *hard*—and he heard moaning, and it was coming from him.

A sharp bark came from behind him. Then another one.

Lauren drew her head back. "Oh, my," she said. "Oh, my."

And he...he had no words. His eyes open, he stared at her, hearing only his speeding heartbeats and his panting breaths, as if he'd run too fast.

"I think I'd better go," she said.

He loosened his grip, and his arms lowered to his sides. She stepped back, then turned. "Let's go, Falco."

She and the dog left, but he stayed in his daughter's bedroom and watched her leave, then listened to their steps on the stairs.

For the first time in three years, he felt fully alive, exhilaration flashing through his veins.

Lauren, he thought. Lauren.

Who would have guessed...?

He should follow her, but he didn't know what to think. His emotions— Okay, his *body* was screaming, *Yes. Hell yes. Just do it, stupid.*

But his mind was still in a state of disbelief, and he didn't want to do anything that would ruin their newly healed friendship.

Behind him, the air vibrated, and it felt to him that there was really a pooka in the room, and it was laughing at him. Instead of turning his head, though, he strode out of the room.

He'd invited her here. The least he could do was to hurry downstairs and get her coat out of the closet and hand it to her.

Six

Ignore rules. Pay attention to kindness.
~Pooka

"I don't know if I said this before, but I'm sorry about Paul."

"Really?" Standing in the front hallway, next to the coat closet, Lauren raised her eyebrows. After that kiss, he brought up her missing husband? *"Really?"*

He hunched his shoulders. "Have you heard anything?"

"Not from him. Not from the sheriff, either."

"So, what are you going to do?"

She sucked in her breath. "I had lunch with my lawyer last week. She reminded me of our prenup. Paul's been missing for over four and a half years and..." She frowned. "I haven't talked to anyone but my lawyer. I wish..." She flipped her hands in the air and looked away from him.

"You wish Noelle were here," he said. "Talk to me. Think of me as her substitute."

She laughed, but it was a broken laugh, and she shook her head.

"A friend, then." His voice was low. "Think of me as a friend."

"A kissing friend."

"The best kind." His left eyebrow crooked up, and he grinned.

She laughed and heard the shakiness, then she took a breath and nodded. "Before Paul disappeared, I'd talked to my lawyer about a possible divorce. She asked if I'd mentioned it to Paul." She stopped, realizing she was shaking.

"Did you?" Adam asked.

"I hadn't yet."

"I know your parents have some money—"

"My grandparents on both sides were doing well. I've already inherited money." She stopped to take a breath. Not just money but stocks and properties, too. But there was no need to tell him everything. "Right now, it's in my name only."

His expression turned grim. "What else did your lawyer say?"

"She thought he might have heard about my meeting with her and could be staying away until the ten years were up in order to get half my money."

"Prenup terms? You think it's possible?"

"Yes and yes, though disappearing for so long is pretty drastic. Paul's ex-wife and I keep in touch. She and their son live in Green Bay. Neither she nor Rodney has heard from him. Rodney's nineteen now, and he and Paul argued often..." She frowned. She'd chosen a husband with her head instead of her heart. The worst mistake of her life. "Anyway, my lawyer advised me to start divorce proceedings. Because he's missing, we have to show proof that we tried to reach him."

"I know you married him in February, but I can't remember the year."

"In February, it will be ten years." Her eyebrows lifted. "And I can't believe you remember the month I'd married."

"I'm good at dates. I remember it had snowed the night before, and I'd plowed for four hours before we drove to the church. That stuck in my head. It was just before Valentine's day, too."

She made a face. Cupid hadn't made it to her wedding. Maybe it was the snow. Though, more likely, it was the groom. "My lawyer's starting the process. We have to prove that we're making a genuine search for him."

"He's been gone for four and a half years. I don't know why you have to prove anything."

"It's the law. I just feel sorry for women who don't have the means that I do. Anyway, my lawyer is starting to prove due diligence."

"What does that mean?"

"It means we get in touch with the sheriff."

He raised his eyebrows.

"Officially," she said. "Not just a phone call. And we have to contact relatives or friends. It's irritating, because we did all of that after he was first missing. No one knew anything. Or if they did, they didn't tell us. But this time, it's official."

"And then what?

"Then we put notices in the Door County Advocate for three weeks in a row."

"And then?"

"If he doesn't show up by then, we can file for divorce. My lawyer says this whole process should take two to three months."

"And if he shows up?"

"My lawyer will take him to court to try to prove he only came back to keep me from divorcing him before the prenup restrictions expire so he can get half my money."

"I hope the piece of shit doesn't show up. I like to think he stumbled into Lake Michigan and drowned."

She shrugged. She didn't want to carry anger around with her. Anger was a bitter taste in her mouth and a twisting in her belly. "My lawyer believes that if we act now, we should make the deadline."

He looked at her for a long moment. "I'd hug you, but I might end up kissing you again."

She looked back at him, her breath caught in her throat before she exhaled shakily, then stepped back, twisted around, and took two steps toward the door...

She halted. Falco took a step farther then turned to look back at her, then sat on his haunches. As if he could see the thoughts churning in her head.

Wasn't this what she wanted? Wanted since she was seventeen?

Yes. Hell yes, it was.

And hadn't the kiss in Tori's bedroom been hot? Amazing? Like a teenage girl's dream?

Better yet, a thirty-five-year-old woman's erotic dream. The beginning of the dream, anyway. And thirty-five-year-old women knew their erotic dream beginnings.

She snapped around, held up her hands, her purse dangling from her elbow.

As if it were choreographed, he stepped forward and lowered his arms, pulling her against him while she went up on her toes. Their bodies were aligned, with her breasts pushed against his chest, and she could feel his erection against her belly. They kissed, their mouths open, as if it were the first, the last, and the only kiss they might ever have. As if it were Christmas and Valentine's Day and the Fourth of July combined. With fireworks exploding above and around and inside them.

Especially inside them.

No man had ever kissed her like this. As if he would die if they stopped.

Or maybe that's how she felt. A small sound of *want* moaned out of her throat, and she lifted a leg to wrap around his thighs—

A bark sounded. *Falco.* She ignored him. Just a few more seconds. Just one more moment. Or two. Two would be better. Or three. Or—

Adam pulled back, breathing heavily. "Tori. That must be her."

She nodded, desire running hot and hotter inside her. The stupid kind of desire that made women do stupid things.

Where were the zero-degree weather and icy pellets when she needed them?

The door was opening, and she broke away from Adam, stepping back and breathing harshly. Tori rushed inside, her cheeks flushed pink and her eyes hazel like Noelle's, sparkling at her. "Lauren!"

Lauren pushed away the disappointment of the interrupted embrace, because what she'd done had not been the smartest thing in the world. Collecting her common sense was no easy task, but she was the Queen of Common Sense, and with her heart still hammering in her chest, she hunched down to kiss Tori.

"I missed you." Tori gripped her.

Lauren straightened, then patted Tori's light brown hair. "Look how pretty you are. And how tall!"

"I'm one of the shortest in my class. I want to be as tall as you."

"You're only twelve," Adam said. At the same time, Lauren said, "Your dad's tall."

"You'll grow," Adam said. At the same time, Lauren said, "You'll probably grow."

"Mom was a shrimp," Tori said as she bent a little to hug Falco.

Lauren glanced at Adam, because that simultaneous talking had been weird. He was looking at her, nodding to give her a go. She turned back to Tori, who was so cute and so like her mom that it made Lauren want to cry because Noelle wasn't here.

"Your mom was only an inch or two below average. And remember how pretty she was. The boys were crazy about her."

"Really?" Tori stood, her eyebrows contracting with suspicion that Lauren was humoring her.

Adam cleared his throat. "I don't think you should be talking to Tori about this."

"Dad! We're having girl talk."

"Yes, Adam," Lauren said. "This is girl talk. Boys butt out."

He narrowed his eyes, and she swallowed a laugh, looking back at Tori.

"I missed you! You should come more..." Tori stopped, her mouth still open as she stepped back. "He *told* you, didn't he?" She sent him a glare so cold it should've frozen him on the spot. "He told you about the big cat. That's why you're here."

"Honey..." She reached out, and Tori took another step back. Lauren dropped her arm. "He did. And he took us upstairs. And guess what?"

"You didn't see it." Tori's tone was flat, the animation gone from her face.

"I didn't," she said. "But..."

She stopped and turned to Adam. His expression was as stony as his daughter's. He didn't look like he wanted her to spill it. That's because he didn't want to believe.

She understood. Neither did she. She glanced down at Falco, who stood at her side again now. She couldn't deny Falco's reaction, but that wasn't proof. Not real proof that she could see and hear.

Even as she thought that, goose bumps rose on her arms.

"Tell her," Adam said, his voice flat.

Lauren turned to Tori and took a deep breath before the words rushed out. "Falco barked at the rug. He's *never* barked at a rug before."

Seven

A laugh is a sound of joy. So is a purr.
~Pooka

As Lauren finished talking, Tori's hands prickled and she felt light-headed. She was not checking her blood, though. This was just the excitement any twelve-year-old would feel when an adult believed her after she'd said something that sounded crazy.

If someone had said the same thing to her, she probably wouldn't believe it.

Unless it was her dad. She'd have to love someone a lot to believe them. That's why her dad believed her. He *wanted* to believe her.

And maybe Lauren loved her a little. But mostly Lauren believed her because of Falco.

Tori turned to Falco, who watched her with his head tilted. As if he were tracking her emotions.

She wouldn't be surprised. Irish wolfhounds were the tallest breed of dogs—she knew that because Lauren had told her so—and maybe that meant they had big brains, too. Stepping forward,

Tori swung her arms around Falco's neck, pushing the side of her head against his as he stood solidly.

"I love you," she whispered, wishing he were her dog. Taking a shivery inhale, she let go and stood, looking at Lauren. "Can I take him upstairs? Can I see what he does?"

"Tori," her dad said in a warning voice.

"Of course," Lauren said at the same time.

"She said yes." Tori squinted at her dad.

"She was just leaving," he said.

Tori rolled her eyes. Most of the time she loved her dad. But sometimes she suspected he wanted to spoil everything she did.

Okay, not *everything*. Just a lot of things.

Sometimes she missed her mom so much that it felt as if there was a giant fist in her chest, squeezing her heart.

"I'm happy to go upstairs with Tori," Lauren said to her dad. "I haven't talked to her for a long time. And of course she wants to see what Falco does with her own eyes."

Tori wanted to say, *Yes!*, but she kept her mouth shut. Her dad wasn't mean, but sometimes he was clueless. And pretty much he was always stubborn. Maybe because he was a man. As much as she loved him, she'd noticed already that most men were more stubborn than most women.

He nodded, and she gave a little skip, and a squeak came out of her mouth. It was only her dad and Lauren, so she didn't feel like a dork. Especially since Lauren was grinning at her.

"Let's go up." Tori spun around and ran

halfway up the steps, hearing Lauren and Falco about five steps behind her. She looked over her shoulder, and her dad was near the bottom. Probably staying back because if he got too close to Falco, the dog might accidentally whack his tail against her dad's face.

But then she saw her dad wasn't watching Falco's butt. He was watching Lauren's.

Ewwww.

As she turned around, thoughts ran through her head, and she wondered what it meant, if it meant anything. Her grandma liked to say all men were dogs. And Grandma didn't mean because men ate fast and farted and liked to lick their private parts, the way dogs did. Tori was old enough to know her grandma meant that men wanted to have sex with women.

But her dad wasn't like that. He wasn't bad-looking. In fact, when he went to school events, single moms and even teachers tried to flirt with him. But he never seemed to notice, and she'd heard one mom tell another that he had a rod stuck up his butt. Lauren had wanted to yell at the mom that her dad still loved her mom, and he would *never* love another woman.

She reached the top step and turned again. This time her dad was looking at Falco, and she exhaled. Only then did she realize she'd been holding her breath.

"Are you okay?" Lauren asked. She was almost at the top of the stairs, and Tori nodded.

Lauren reached forward and wiped the pad of her index finger across Tori's cheekbone. Lifting her finger so Tori could see the moistness on the pad of her finger, she murmured, "Why the tear?"

Lauren's eyes were sad, and her forehead was crumpled with concern. Tori's throat tightened, and she shook her head. Unable to speak, she shuffled back so Lauren and Falco could step into the hallway, and behind them her dad. She hurried into her bedroom to grab a tissue and blow her nose. But she stopped instead.

Pooka wasn't on the rug.

"*Here.* I'm here."

Tori whipped her head around—and there was the pooka. On Tori's bed, her neck up, watching her.

"Show-and-tell time again?" Pooka asked.

A footstep headed into the room, a dull thump on her wooden floor. Lauren. Behind her was Falco, and then her dad.

Lauren gestured to the fuzzy rug with her hand. The place Tori's dad was staring at. "Go on," Lauren said to Falco. "Go and say hi to the big cat."

Falco stepped toward the direction that Lauren had gestured. Tori put her hand over her mouth, holding back a cry. And then Falco turned toward the bed, stopping right where Pooka's head was.

Falco *ruffed*. Not a bark or a growl, just a low noise that acknowledged the big cat.

Tori switched her gaze to her dad and Lauren. "This is where Pooka is now."

"What's the pooka doing there?" her dad asked.

Tori looked from Pooka to her father. "I didn't ask, but I think she wanted to nap on my bed. So she did."

"You said she's a cat," Lauren said. "Cats like soft spots."

"A pooka." Her dad shook his head. "A *cat* pooka."

Tori rolled her eyes.

"But still a cat," Lauren said in her clear voice, "and if she's like most cats, she'll do what she wants to do."

Her dad's mouth set, but he didn't argue. Probably because Lauren was right.

Something bubbled up inside Tori. Something...unfamiliar. She didn't know for sure what it was, so she put her hand over her mouth to stop it. But it bubbled out of her mouth, and the sound felt raw and uneven. But there was no denying what it was.

A giggle. She was giggling.

How could this be? She laughed sometimes. Of course, she did. But when she did, it was a fast burst of laughter. Like a "ha ha ha," and that was it. But this...

She dropped her hand, because the giggles were like a volcano overflowing inside her. And her cheeks... They were wet. What was wrong with them?

Then Lauren was there. Kneeling down, her knees on the carpet. Tori bent over her, as if she'd been pulled to Lauren. She wrapped her arms around Lauren's neck, and Lauren wrapped her arms around her back. Though Lauren wasn't her mom, and for sure was nothing at all like her mom, it felt good as Lauren just hugged her. Just held on. And she just held on back.

A bigger hand rubbed her back. Her dad. Not saying anything, just rubbing her back.

The giggles were stopped already. The tears

stopped in another minute, and she was just breathing harsh breaths. In yet another minute, she straightened, her dad's hand falling off as she scrubbed the tears from her face, then headed to her desk in the corner, the one her dad had found on the edge of Highway 42. He'd dragged and somehow pulled it into the back of his pickup, then taken it home, painted it turquoise, and put a mirror on it.

She grabbed a tissue now, blew her nose, then she looked in the mirror. Tears still glittered in her eyes, and, behind her, she saw Lauren and her dad both peering at her face in the mirror with identical expressions of anxiety.

At the side of the bed, there was movement. Falco. His head bending closer to Pooka's face.

Then she heard a hiss. Still looking in the mirror, she saw Pooka's front right leg slash out at Falco's muzzle.

Falco yelped and jumped back as Tori spun around. "Pooka scratched Falco's face. I saw it!"

Lauren was already at Falco's side, bending to inspect the side of his mouth as he whimpered. "He's bleeding. Oh, my God, he's bleeding." She looked at Tori's dad, her mouth gaped open. "This has to be proof that the pooka is real. It's really real."

"Shit," her dad said, and he never swore in front of Tori. "Oh, shit."

"We can't tell anyone," Lauren said, her arm still wrapped around Falco's neck. Her dad and Lauren stared at each other for another moment, then turned at the same time to look at her.

Her father raked his fingers through his thick

hair, which Tori only noticed because a couple of her friends' fathers were going bald already. "We won't tell anyone."

Tori's chest squeezed. "We're having a secret," she said, and her voice sound funny, like it was rusty. "All three of us are having a secret."

"If you include the dog and the pooka," Lauren said in her matter-of-fact voice, "it's five."

"You're counting the dog and the pooka?" Tori's dad looked at Lauren, his mouth curved up. "That doesn't sound like you."

Lauren shrugged. "Falco talked to her, whether you believe it or not."

"I did believe it." He looked at Tori. "Didn't I?"

She nodded, tears prickling her eyes again, because it was true. And she knew it wasn't that he wanted to believe there was a giant, invisible pooka in her bedroom. He wanted to believe *her*.

"No one else will believe it," Lauren went on. "But here's Falco's bleeding mouth. I don't see how we can ignore that."

Tori kept her mouth shut. She didn't remember everything her mom said, but she remembered once that her mom said Lauren loved her dog more than she loved most humans. That didn't surprise Tori. If she had a dog, she would love it like that. Dogs were easier to love than people. Easier than cats, too—though she would never say it to the pooka.

"That's right." Tori narrowed her eyes at her dad. Sometimes he just didn't get it. "And just because Falco is a dog, that doesn't mean he's not as smart as humans. I think he's even smarter than a couple of my teachers."

"I don't know about your teachers," Lauren said. "But he certainly has a better heart than most humans." She bent to kiss the top of Falco's head, then held his head close against her chest, not seeming to care that drops of blood might stain her sweater.

Her actions made Tori feel that it wasn't weird for her to talk to a giant cat that no one else could see. Made her feel that this wasn't a dream. Or, worse, that it wasn't a diabetic coma, and she would wake up in a hospital.

Or a morgue.

She tried to stop thoughts like these, the ones that made her think she wasn't going to be here long, but they kept haunting her.

"I can't believe I'm saying this," Adam said, "but if the cat scratched the dog, it could scratch Tori."

"Dad, the pooka would never—"

A meow of what was clearly a protest ripped through the room, and Tori snapped around, her eyes opening wide. "Pooka!"

But Pooka's eyes were already closed, her head down on her front legs. As if she were tired of listening to people.

Tori turned to her dad. "Pooka would never do that. Never."

He was rubbing his jaw, not saying anything. There was silence as she stared at him, and after a moment his hand dropped from his jaw and he sighed and nodded his head. "Okay," he said. "Okay."

She nodded, too, even as he wondered how he could've made Pooka leave. How could you make someone you couldn't see go away?

Lauren straightened. "Falco and I have to get going."

"Already?" Tori held out her hands. "But—"

"Tori." Her dad's voice was harsh.

Pulling her hands back, she supposed she could cry and yell, but he was right, and she would just say stuff she shouldn't.

As the others headed into the hall, she peeked over at Pooka, but she looked to be in a deep nap. Tori didn't know why Pooka had come into her life if all she did was sleep.

Frowning, she went downstairs behind Lauren and Falco and her dad.

It felt like a funeral procession.

When they reached the bottom of the stairs, her dad took Lauren's coat out of the closet, and he helped her put it on. He never did things like that, not even for Grandma, and Tori watched him being careful to hold the coat sleeves at just the right height for Lauren to put her arms in them.

He *did* like Lauren. He *did*. First he'd stared at her butt, and now this.

At least Tori thought it meant he liked Lauren. It was hard to tell about boys.

She wasn't sure about Lauren, either. Her expression was pleasant, but there was tension on her face.

Was that a good thing? When Josh was nearby, Tori felt tension. Lauren was lifting her chin and her nose in the air now, and Tori didn't do *that*. When Josh was near, she looked away or even down at her shoes, knowing that she would say the wrong thing or trip over her words.

It wasn't that she *liked* him.

Well, maybe a little. But that was stupid, because he was in ninth grade, and at school, she'd seen him talking to a girl in ninth grade who had long hair and big boobs. Everyone knew that boys liked big boobs.

Hers were tiny. How could she compete with that? And besides her age and her underdeveloped breasts, there was her type one diabetes. Though Josh was nice to her most of the time, a boy like him wouldn't want someone like her.

Not that she wanted a boyfriend. Not Josh or any other boy.

She didn't know what she wanted.

Lauren's coat was on now. Tori's dad stepped back, and Lauren turned slightly to hug her again. "It's okay," Lauren said, hugging her. "I know what happened must feel odd. Maybe you should talk to a counselor at—"

"I'm not talking to anybody." Tori's voice rose to a squeak. "They'll think I'm nuts. They'll probably think it's something to do with the diabetes. None of them will believe me."

"Okay. You don't have to tell anyone." She looked at Tori's dad for confirmation.

So did Tori, and he nodded.

Lauren turned back, still holding her, still gripping her arms. "I promise it's going to be okay."

Tori looked into her eyes. Lauren was saying stuff that doctors said on TV about her living a long, long time.

But sometimes on TV, in the last scene, Tori thought, the patient died.

"One more hug," Lauren said, "then I have to go." She didn't wait for permission but hugged her again. And then kept hugging her, holding her close for a long moment.

It felt good. Really good. Tori raised her arms to hold Lauren just as close, and thoughts buzzed through her head. Her gaze caught her dad's, and he was looking at her and Lauren as if someone had slugged him in his belly.

Her breath sucked in. Maybe her dad was looking at them and thinking it should be her mom hugging her.

But his sad look, as if someone had stolen his autographed football by Aaron Rogers—the way he looked when Tori knew he was thinking about her mom—wasn't there.

This time, he was just looking as if someone had shot a Taser at him. Like he was stunned and waiting for his senses to return to his brain.

So maybe that look meant her dad really liked Lauren. If he did...well, it might be okay. Lauren wasn't like her mom, but Tori didn't want someone just like her mom. That would be icky.

And even though Lauren was married, her husband had disappeared years ago. Everyone thought for sure that he was dead. Just a few weeks ago, Tori had heard two teachers gossiping about it in the library. One of them had said she'd like to kill her insurance agent, and the other one had laughed.

Maybe it was wicked, but Tori hoped Lauren's husband was dead. Her mom hadn't liked him much. She hadn't said it out loud, but even though Tori had been only nine when her mom died, she could tell. Maybe someone would find his body somewhere real soon. And then Lauren and her dad would get married.

Tori would like that a lot. There had to be a way she could get Lauren and her dad together. She didn't know yet but—

Her wandering thoughts braked to a halt.

Pooka would know. Pooka would help her. After all, there must be a reason the pooka had come to Trouble Bay besides napping on her rug and now her bed.

Tori just had to find out what the pooka's reason was. Right now.

Eight

Sometimes humans remind me of mewling kittens. Other times they're like angry wolves about to attack. ~Pooka

"I'm not as thickheaded as my daughter thinks," Adam said in the front hall.

Lauren looked at him with her lips tight, clearly holding back a laugh while he held back a groan.

He'd done it again. This man-woman thing had been much easier when he was nineteen and ran into Noelle at the beach, and she smiled at him, and he smiled back. The next thing he was buying her ice cream and inviting her to kayak with him, and that was it.

The love of his life.

And then she'd died.

Damn drunken tourist who was alive and would be out of jail soon. People said to Adam that at least the asshole had had insurance. As if money healed the ache inside him and could give his daughter a mother. As if Noelle's life was worth money.

A hand on his shoulder stopped his thoughts.

He blinked and saw he was staring at Lauren's concerned face. He fought a mad desire to put his lips against hers for the third time today.

To kiss her until they were breathless.

To drag her into the coat closet.

To close the door behind them and—

"Are you all right?" Lauren asked.

He shook his head. He had a hard-on. If she glanced down, she would see that bulge.

This was like high school, when he would sometimes have to hold a notebook over the front of his jeans.

"I'm okay." His voice croaked, and her eyebrows rose.

"Are you thinking about the pooka?" she asked. "It is hard to believe."

He still stared at her. Straight into her eyes. And he realized she was staring into his eyes, too. As if she wanted to drown in his gaze.

And he wanted to drown in hers.

Or her kiss.

Definitely her kiss.

This was trouble.

But maybe he was ready for trouble. Trouble in Trouble Bay.

"Right now I'm not thinking much at all."

"I'd better go." She backed up, but Falco stayed where he was, his tail wagging, his jaws open, giving Adam a doggy smile.

"Falco looks like he wants to stay." A lightness started inside him. As if the heavy weight he'd been carrying for the last three years was slipping off his back.

"This is ridiculous." She frowned down at Falco, then lifted her head and frowned at him. "And strange." She added a scowl to the frown. "Do you think the pooka did something to him?"

He stared at her face with the fine bones and high cheekbones. The paleness and the beauty. "Do you believe in spells?"

"I believe in spelling tests."

"Not that kind. Witches' spells. Pooka spells."

"No. People do what they want to do."

"Neither do I." He took a step closer to her. He couldn't ever remember being so attracted to a woman. Not even Noelle. Of course, he'd been crazy about Noelle. But it had been a lighter crazy. Sunlight and blue skies.

This crazy was different. Darker. Thicker. Lusher.

Crazy as if there was magic in the house. Black magic. White magic. Red-hot magic.

Maybe there was. Maybe it was the pooka.

Or maybe it was just Lauren.

She stared at him, as if mesmerized.

Good. It was only fair since he was mesmerized, too. "Yet I have a strong desire to kiss you again."

Her eyes widened.

"I didn't have it before you came into my house."

"Isn't that usual?" she asked. "To have someone in the vicinity before you think about kissing her?"

"Not always. Not when that switch was turned off."

"Seriously? I recall a few women hitting on you at Noelle's funeral."

"I've always been a one-woman man. And then I saw you today." He clamped his mouth shut. A fire that hadn't been burning for the last three years had suddenly flared up, but he didn't think she'd appreciate the analogy.

"Well, you're a man," she said. "Men do think about sex often. Maybe it's just...time."

He didn't reply right away, still looking at her face. Forcing himself not to look down farther.

But she looked down, directly at the zipper of his jeans. At his bulge.

Her head snapped up, her lips parted.

Surprise, surprise, he thought. And the look in her eyes...so vulnerable when he never thought of her as vulnerable. That look touched him. Warmed him. This woman who had been his wife's best friend and who was helping his daughter and him. Who had lost her husband, making them two of a kind.

"Or maybe it's just you." The roughness of his voice echoed the way his body felt.

He stepped forward, and she didn't step back.

Bending slightly, he kissed her again. Their third kiss. As their lips met and she made a small moan, a creak on the stairway's top tread made him pull his arms away from her and step back.

She tottered backward, falling on her butt on the wooden floor.

She didn't say a word, staring up at him.

Falco growled.

Tori rushed down the stairs, her feet in her fuzzy slippers sounding like combat boots. And he still stared at Lauren as she struggled to get up.

One second he'd been thinking about Noelle.

The next he'd been all over Lauren. Straight-laced Lauren, his wife's best friend and his daughter's godmother. Lauren, who was looking at him with disillusionment in her eyes.

She pushed up to her feet, and he stepped forward, holding out his hands as Tori reached the bottom landing.

"What happened?" Tori asked, her voice pitched high with worry. "Did you fall, Lauren?"

"I'm okay." Her lips twisted. Glancing down at the hands he still held out, she pinched her lips together and took a step back before she turned to Tori. "I fell, and then I got up. Not a big deal."

"How did you fall?"

"It happens sometimes," Lauren said. "Sometimes you just do something stupid."

Tori's forehead crinkled.

"Don't worry about it." Lauren brushed her thumb over Tori's forehead. "Sometimes it's good to do stupid things. It teaches you not to do it again."

"What stupid thing could you be doing?"

Lauren laughed, a discordant sound that she stopped abruptly. "Just took a wrong step. That's all. I have to go now. It was great seeing you." She bent to hug her.

"You, too." Tori put her chin over Lauren's shoulder and closed her eyes, holding on tightly. They stayed like that for a minute, with Tori's forehead scrunched, and Adam was sure that Lauren's forehead was scrunched, too.

As for him, he felt like his gut was twisted. He wanted to fall on his knees. He wanted to pray. And not to God. He wanted to pray to Noelle.

And he wanted to pray to Lauren.

Maybe to God, too, though he wasn't sure if he believed. Mostly he wanted to pray for salvation.

And he wanted to pray for a chance to have sex with Lauren.

Because he was like a dead man coming to life again. Rebirth. And rebirth came with pain. Even a stupid male like him knew that. And what represented life more than sex?

And he didn't want it with any woman. Just Lauren. The woman he'd dropped onto the floor. The woman he hadn't helped to rise until it was too late.

He watched her and Falco leave the house, the front door closing behind them.

"Daddy, what did you do?" Tori's voice rose with every word, and he finally looked away from the closed door.

Words seemed to be stuck in his throat, and he shook his head.

Her underlip pushed out, and she stomped one slippered foot on the wooden floor. "I hate you. You ruin *everything*."

Then she was running away from him, running up the stairs. He watched her, feeling inside like he was the breaker of hearts. Only the heart that was breaking wasn't Lauren's. It was his daughter's. And it was his own.

Something brushed his leg, and he didn't look at it.

It happened again, but his time it bumped the arm hanging at his side.

He glanced down...and nothing was there. "Pooka?" he asked, and he didn't feel foolish for saying it. Too busy feeling like a fool for the way he'd treated Lauren.

Why had he done it? He'd wanted her.

And then he'd heard his daughter on the stairs, and he'd felt guilty. Not because he was kissing Lauren. After all, it had been a little over three years since Noelle passed. He could have had interludes during the three years. Just to make him feel alive. But it had never felt right.

And with Lauren, it wouldn't be an interlude. With Lauren, it would be real. Maybe too real.

Even as he thought that much, as if his derailed-by-lust brain cells were on track again and connecting, sharp teeth bit the top of his left hand. He yelped, and he thought he heard a cat's squawk.

Looking down at the top of his hand, he saw drops of blood.

His skin chilled. He had to be imagining it.

But how could he imagine blood?

He couldn't. No more than he'd imagined the kisses. And no more than he'd imagined Lauren's response.

Once again, his world was turning upside down. About the only thing he was sure of right now was that he wasn't going to get much sleep tonight.

What if the pooka bit Tori? If it did, how could he protect her from an invisible animal?

Still watching his hand, he saw the drops of blood drying up. Disappearing.

He blinked. When he looked again, the tiny bite marks on his skin were healed. Gone.

As if he'd never been scratched.

As if there were no pooka...

Or was there?

He'd seen what he'd seen, he'd felt what he'd felt, but now the proof was gone, and he wasn't sure of anything anymore.

Nine

Nothing feels as good as curling up in a patch of sunlight. ~Pooka

One and a half weeks later

Every walk for Darryl was a walk of shame. That's what happened when you were a big man. Big as in overweight. A lot of weight. He was honest with himself. He was fat. Obese. Not chubby. He was a good hundred pounds over chubby.

And a hospital... That was always bad, because he could see the nurses and the aides look at him, and he knew they were thinking, *Oh, no. Hell no. I don't want to take care of that. It will take four of us to lift him.*

Christ, he was sweating already. His walk slowed until he was shuffling, and he realized he was on the wrong side of the hospital. Lauren Finney's offices would be in the administrative wing. Probably somewhere in the back with a better view. He should ask someone, but he didn't want to talk to anyone. Not the way they looked at him, as if he were a leper.

He slowed. Coming here was a mistake. He hadn't made an appointment with Lauren, but after the visit from the muscled guy wearing a leather jacket and black pleated pants—looking like a detective in a TV show—Darryl's emotions had overwhelmed him. Stupidly, he'd called Piper, his half-sister, and now she was a wreck.

All of this was making him sick. He should have done something earlier. He shouldn't have allowed it to go so far.

Now that it was done, how could he undo it?

He didn't have an appointment with a client until this afternoon, so he'd left the office, locking it behind him, then had stuffed himself into his SUV and had driven to the hospital.

Was this why Lauren had missed the phone call two days ago on the first of the month?

How could she do this without telling him?

She was ruining everything.

It was cold out. November already. Not freezing yet during the day, though that could change anytime, any hour. He wore his voluminous plaid coat over his white shirt, blue tie, and navy slacks, and he wasn't cold. If anything, he was running hot. That's what the extra weight did. That's what anger and fear and worry did.

He turned, and a middle-aged black woman wearing a long-sleeved top with cartoon animals and blue-gray scrub pants stopped. She put her hand on his arm. She had a worried expression and a kind face.

"Sir, can I help you? Are you lost?"

He shook his head. "I'm fine. I'm just, uh, on the wrong floor." He hurried away, hoping she didn't think it was because of the color of her skin. No, it was because her kindness made him want to cry.

His world was falling apart. Nothing he would say to Lauren Finney would change that.

He'd done something stupid, and now it was too late to fix it. He wanted to blame Lauren, but he couldn't buy it.

Still, she had everything, and he had nothing. *They* had nothing. His mother and Piper didn't have a life. He couldn't even blame Lauren for talking to her lawyer about divorcing Finney. Finney hadn't deserved her. He hadn't deserved loyalty from Darryl, either. If he could have found another job, he would have left long ago.

He didn't know what had happened to Finney. He suspected foul play, but the list of people with grievances against Finney must be long.

Still, none of that helped him.

If it were just him who would be hurt by the truth, he'd be honest with Lauren. He would tell her what he'd done. He would be willing to go to jail.

After all, what kind of a life did he have anyway?

But it wasn't just him. He had a mother and sister who counted on him. They were the reasons he'd taken that money. Always planning on returning it...until the amount grew and grew, and he had to admit that restitution would never happen.

If he went to prison...

Sweating and huffing like he'd run a 54K race, he stopped behind two people waiting for the elevator, the down light on. Sweat ran down his back, his underarms, and every place on his body that sweated.

No way could he do that to Piper and his mother.

He had to do something. He didn't want to, but he had no choice.

"Hello, Darryl."

The precisely spoken voice sent panic into his throat, and he looked at the thin woman with the tall dog at her side, and his heart pumped wildly inside his chest.

"Darryl?"

Oh, God. Oh, Jesus. Oh, shit.

He swallowed and sweat prickled beneath his underarms. "Uh, Lauren. Good to see you." *Should he mention the visit today from the guy who'd said he was from her lawyer's office? Oh, God. This was so horrible.*

"Are you visiting anyone?"

"Uh, yes! A friend. Appendicitis."

"I hope your friend is doing all right."

"She's recovering well," he said, forcing himself to sound calm. He was an insurance agent. Smiling and sounding knowledgeable and likable was what he did for a living. He was the jolly fat man. Harmless. Friendly. Reliable.

And that was all the truth. His other self

wasn't his true self. It was a new self born of desperation. One who stole and lied and was trying to think of ways to get out of it... And the only way out that came to him made him want to throw up the burrito he'd stopped to gobble down on the way here.

"I'm taking Falco to the children's ward," Lauren said.

"Uh, he's a therapy dog, huh? Isn't he too big?" Even as he said that, he cringed, imagining she must be thinking about his girth. And the dog had on a red vest that said THERAPY DOG in big letters, so that made him a double idiot.

"No, the kids love him, and he loves them, too." Her head tilted. "Are you sure you're okay?"

The elevator dinged, and people walked out. He looked toward it. A woman was on crutches, and behind her was someone in a wheelchair.

It was going to take a minute or two for them to get out and him to get in. A short time, but it seemed like an eon to him.

"There's a bench over there." She pointed behind him. "Would you like to sit down?"

"I'm okay. I just, uh, feel bad for my friend." He heard a crack and looked behind him. The wheelchair hit something, and another man was going inside to turn the chair around. Shit, shit, shit. This was taking forever. Meanwhile, words were backing up in his mind, eager to pour out of his mouth, even though he shut his lips and clamped down his teeth.

He was *not* going to say anything. It would be a stupid thing to do.

He took a deep breath, and with his mouth

open, the dreaded words popped out. "I had a visitor today who said your lawyer sent him. That you need to show you've searched for Paul before you file for divorce."

She nodded, her lips pressed together, her shoulders hitched up.

He shouldn't question her. He really shouldn't say anything.

"Why now?" he asked.

Her face closed. The people waiting for the elevator moved forward, but he stood where he was, as if his shoes were planted on the floor, and she remained standing, too.

"I'm doing this on the advice of my lawyer. I have to go now." She turned, and she and her dog walked away, no doubt to make some children feel better.

As he watched her, he just felt an immense sadness. He knew about the prenup. Paul had mentioned it a few times, and not happily.

They were married in February. Just before Valentine's Day. The day to celebrate love and romance. Paul was the most calculating and least romantic person Darryl knew, which was why it had stuck in his head.

Though Paul's body hadn't been found, Darryl suspected he was dead. Darryl hadn't committed murder, but he'd committed another crime. Sooner or later, he would have to pay the consequences, but he'd always hoped it would be later.

This really messed things up for him. He couldn't stand to have any changes. Not for himself so much. For Piper and his mother.

There had to be *something* he could do. But he could only think of one thing. One horrible thing.

His legs shaking, he stepped up to the elevators and pressed the down button. He was sweating again. Right now, he wished for below-freezing weather. Right now, he felt as if he were in the bowels of hell.

Ten

Changes are opportunities.
~Pooka

Lauren was frowning when she and Falco stepped out of the elevator toward her office. Her favorite times at the hospital were her visits to the children's ward with Falco. The children loved her big dog. There were always smiles and happy faces, and normally she carried back some of the smiles inside her.

Not this time. How odd to run into Darryl. Everyone had to go to the hospital sometime. But he was a terrible liar, and she didn't believe for one second that he'd been visiting a friend.

It wasn't hard to guess the real reason he was here. He'd been nervous and unhappy. Sweating. His face red and mottled. His breathing was rasping. He was obviously having trouble catching his breath.

She wasn't a doctor or a nurse, but even she could see that something was very wrong with his health. Since he considered her, in effect, his boss, he was afraid to tell her. She couldn't force him to tell her, but she would call him and remind him that he was entitled to sick days and he should take care of himself.

Better yet, since he was obviously uncomfortable talking to her, she would email him.

She reached her office, the door a polished walnut. The offices, her assistant's and then hers, were tasteful, but nothing too expensive-looking. She hadn't refused the big office—that would have been silly, and if she wasn't using it, someone else would. But she didn't want or need the heavy, opulent furniture, preferring streamlined yet comfortable furnishings. If any donors stopped by her office, she didn't want them to get the wrong message. It was embarrassing.

Her assistant for the last four years, Ashleigh, greeted her. Ashleigh had reddish-brown hair and was on the short side, with the kind of curves that men liked. She had gotten married last spring, but she was writing a book on how to flirt, and had already decided that when it was done, she would publish it herself.

"Your friend called again," Ashleigh said.

"What friend?"

"You know. The contractor." Ashleigh sighed. "There's something sexy about a man who works with his hands."

"And there's something smart about an assistant who works."

"Are you calling him?" Ashleigh asked, not fazed by her reply.

"No." Lauren headed to her office. The door

was open, and Falco lunged ahead of her, heading straight to his water bowl.

"Why not?"

"Why should I?" Lauren slowed and looked behind her.

"Do I have to spell it out?" Ashleigh crossed her legs and leaned back in her chair. "He's called every day for over a week. He sounds sorry and desperate. I don't know what he did to piss you off, but it's times like this that men will promise anything. It's times like this that a girl can't pass up."

"It's not what you think."

Ashleigh raised her eyebrows.

"It's nothing. We just kissed." And then he'd let her go. As if she had cooties. And she'd fallen on her butt.

"I don't believe you." Ashleigh narrowed her eyes. "When you kiss a man, it means *something*. Call him. See him. Give him another kiss, and then come here and tell me again that it was *just a kiss* and meant nothing."

"Who's the boss in this office?"

"Who knows more about men?"

"Who's older and was married longer than you?"

"Who married a man she didn't love?"

Lauren sucked in her breath. She felt as if someone had socked her.

"Oh, shit. I shouldn't have said that." Ashleigh uncrossed her legs and held out her hands. "I just want you to be happy, and I have a feeling about this. I know it hurt you when Paul went missing, but—"

"No."

"No? It didn't hurt you?"

"It embarrassed me." She shrugged. It felt good to tell the truth. "I was thinking of divorcing him."

"Did he know?"

"I hadn't mentioned it."

"But might he have guessed?"

"It's possible." She heard the dryness of her voice. "My lawyer thinks so, but I'm not sure. He had a big ego."

"And a small heart?"

Lauren's lips twisted, but she didn't say anything.

"So I guess he didn't hurt you," Ashleigh said. "What about this guy? Adam? Could he hurt you?"

Lauren frowned, not comfortable with this question. She knew she didn't have to answer, but... "Yes," she said with a sigh.

"Then take a chance. You care for him. If you don't take the chance, you might be sorry for the rest of your life. It might be the biggest mistake you make."

"I don't know..." Lauren shook her head, speaking slowly. "He hurt me already. How can you be sure that a man won't hurt you again?"

The corners of Ashleigh's lips turned down. "You can never be sure."

"That's what I thought." Lauren half turned toward her office.

"He's going to hurt you," Ashleigh said, her words ringing. "But you're going to hurt him, too. That's what happens when people care for each other. That's what happens when you're in love."

"No one said anything about love." Lauren stepped inside her office and closed the door, not waiting for a reply, but her heart was pounding, and she wondered, if the same thing had happened between her and any other man, would she have been so hurt?

The answer came swiftly. A big, fat *NO*.

She would have considered his grief and would have commiserated with him.

And she did commiserate. After all, she'd loved Noelle, too. She still missed Noelle, too.

And she was scared, too. Very scared.

What if she allowed herself to see him again? What if more kissing ensued? And even more than kissing ensued?

There was a pen on her desktop. She sat behind the desk and gripped the pen.

She didn't want to be hurt.

But did she want to live her life in fear of getting hurt?

Her parents hadn't loved her. She'd always known that. They were people who didn't love deeply. Maybe at all. As if their senses were dulled.

Paul hadn't loved her, though he'd said he did. She'd known that, and she hadn't loved him, either. Marrying him had been safe.

Dull.

Unsatisfying.

She had thought that was what she wanted. What she should be satisfied with. She wasn't like Noelle and the other girls. Her parents had taught her that marriage was a partnership, and love was an ephemeral emotion, just like any other emotion. One moment it was there, and the next moment it was gone.

She took a deep breath. Maybe later she would call Adam and calmly tell him that she wasn't upset about anything. But for now she needed to get to work.

Four hours later, the phone buzzed. She picked it up, and it wasn't Ashleigh. It was Adam.

She gave the wall between her office and Ashleigh's desk a scowl. Her assistant was probably chortling after transferring the call without her go-ahead.

"Hello, Adam, I'm fine, and you have nothing to apologize for. I understand and—"

"Come to dinner tonight."

She sat up straight.

"I'm making chicken," he continued. "It's my mother's recipe. I know I screwed up, but Tori wants to see you. Come for her."

She frowned. "I don't think this is a good idea. I'd like to see Tori sometime. Maybe I could take her shopping."

"You said you didn't hold anything against me."

She made a face. Yes, she had said that. She'd lied. She opened her mouth to say no, but the words didn't come out. She kept thinking of what Ashleigh had said.

What if Ashleigh was right? What if not taking a chance would be something she would regret for the rest of her life?

She took a deep breath. He wasn't saying anything, and the silence was stretching out, growing uncomfortable.

"Yes," she said. "Yes, I'll come."

It might be a mistake, but why not make mistakes? Wasn't that what life was about? Learning through mistakes?

Her father used to say that mistakes were for people who weren't careful enough.

She'd been careful all her life, and none of it had brought her love.

None of it had brought her children.

Or happiness.

Maybe it was time for her to practice a little carelessness and see what happened. Just as an experiment.

Eleven

Selfishness can be a virtue.
~Pooka

Upstairs in the hall, Tori hadn't meant to listen in on her dad's conversation with Lauren on the land phone they'd had for what seemed like forever. She'd picked it up in the hallway at the same time as her dad had picked it up downstairs, and he'd spoken first.

She didn't feel bad about not putting down the phone. She was a kid, not an angel. After Lauren had left their house last week, she'd hoped that... Well, she'd had hopes. And they hadn't come true.

But now Lauren was coming to dinner. Yay! Tori hung up the phone and hurried into her bedroom, laughing breathlessly.

Pooka was sleeping on the bed again, curled up, though there wasn't much of a patch of sunlight. The school bus had dropped Tori off only twenty minutes ago, and it was already dark out. Sometimes she thought of the sun like a big light in the sky, and she wished it would get some new batteries. But today she wasn't going to whine about stuff she couldn't change. She was happy right now, and when she was happy, she wanted everyone to be happy.

Even the pooka.

"Wakey, wakey," she said.

The giant cat's head lay on the pillow toward the window, with only one closed eye showing. She opened her eye now, her displeasure clear. It seemed to Tori that Pooka could say more with one blue eye than humans said with a bunch of words.

Tori giggled. Having Pooka around was like having an older sister. Only her sister had soft fur, whiskers, a tail, and four legs. And she didn't wear any of Tori's clothes. If this were a math question, the answer would be *sisters zero, pookas one hundred.*

"If there was an Olympic contest for sleeping animals," Tori said, "you would win. Hands down."

"Yesss." Pooka stretched. In the past few weeks, Tori had discovered that Pooka loved to be admired. Not like that was a shocker. Who didn't like being admired? She did. And for sure, so did Bethany in her class, who wore makeup and tight tops to show that she had bigger breasts than any other girl in their grade.

But Tori didn't care about Bethany. What did she want big breasts for that bounced all over the place? And for sure she didn't want boys looking at them. The thought made her stomach feel funny, and she squished it. Right now, she had good things to think about. Right now, her dad was happy. She'd heard it in his voice.

She was happy, too.

"She's coming!" Tori plonked her butt down on the mattress, bouncing a little. "She's coming!"

"I knew that."

"If you know, then who am I talking about?"

"Are you trying to trip me up?" Pooka's tone was amused. "Lauren, of course."

"Do you know *everything*?"

Pooka didn't answer immediately, staring at her. Sometimes Tori wondered if the pooka wasn't real. Maybe she was a computer-generated creature. An AI someone had sent to her bedroom. Artificial Intelligence.

Tori didn't believe it, not really. It wasn't just that she didn't want to believe it, but when she touched Pooka, she was warm like a real cat, and her fur was soft like a real cat's.

And what about the time the pooka had met Falco? She'd clawed his muzzle and he'd bled. Just a couple drops, but they'd been real drops. That meant she was real.

Her dad had thought so, too. Before she'd gone to bed that night, he was worried that Pooka might scratch her. As if that would happen. She'd had to promise that Pooka wouldn't harm her. Which was kind of freaky, because she wasn't sure if he completely believed that Pooka was real.

"I don't know everything," Pooka said now. "Sometimes I make educated guesses. I give them percentages."

"What was the percentage of my last question?"

"Ninety-nine point ninety-eight." Still curled up, Pooka turned her head so that both blue eyes looked at her like she was seeing inside Tori's head and could read her thoughts. "I saw them kiss."

"You were downstairs when they kissed?"

"They kissed in your bedroom. But don't you know by now that I can be anywhere I want to be?"

"You watch us all the time?"

Pooka shuddered. "Only in my nightmares."

Suddenly cold, Tori crossed her arms. "Sometimes I think you don't like humans."

"I like you. You let me sleep on your bed at night."

"Ha! I let you *hog* my bed at night." Tori felt warm again. Happy again. Sometimes the pooka acted like an annoying older sister. "If you know so much, what are we having for dinner tonight?"

"I'm ninety-nine-point-nine percent sure that dessert will be cherry pie."

Tori giggled. Cherry pie was her dad's favorite. Hers, too. Most people thought that anyone with type one diabetes couldn't have desserts with sugar—and what kind of really good desserts didn't have sugar? But that wasn't true. She could have a small serving. She just had to be careful.

It wasn't always fun, but she was alive. Being dead or sick or in a coma would be less fun.

After her mom had been killed in the car accident, Tori had thought that maybe she wouldn't mind being dead. Her mom had believed in life after death. They'd had long talks about it when she was young, and her dad was in the Marine Corps.

She suspected now that her mom had been preparing her in case her dad was hurt or killed.

No one had thought it would be her mom.

She shivered. Cold again. After her mom's funeral, she'd felt like she had a big hole in her heart, and the hole never filled up.

Sometimes she'd thought of calling Lauren, but it would have felt odd to do it when she knew her dad didn't want her to do it. She wasn't sure why, but now that she was older, almost a teenager, she thought maybe when she asked Lauren for advice it made him feel like he wasn't doing a good enough job of being a dad. And not just a dad but a mom, too. That had to be even harder.

And then the pooka had appeared, and at almost the same time, Lauren had come back into her life.

"Your mom was always there for you," Pooka said, bringing Tori's attention back to her.

Tori stared. "You mean..."

"After the accident? Oh, yes. Neither you nor your father were ready to let her go."

"And we're ready now?"

Pooka's eyes closed. "Maybe."

"Do you have the percentage of this, too?"

"There are three people involved. Too many variables."

Tori let go of her knees and gave another little butt jump on the mattress. Three people. That must mean Lauren. And not just Lauren alone. But Lauren and her dad. Because that made two.

And there was her, too. She made three.

She put her lips together, holding back a happy squeal. She was happy that Lauren was coming...

And she was scared.

"What are the odds that this time my dad doesn't ruin it?" she asked.

No answer came, and when she looked down, she saw that Pooka's eyes were closed. Either she was sleeping or just pretending to.

Tori rolled up so her back was against the cat's and closed her eyes. She suspected the pooka just didn't want to admit twice that she didn't know.

In that way, pookas were a lot like adults.

Twelve

If I were a human, I would dance every hour of every day. The rest of the time, I would sleep and eat. *~Pooka*

"She's here!" Tori called out.

In the kitchen, taking the wine out of the fridge, Adam heard Tori's shout. His hand jerked, and his grasp tightened on the bottle. Part of his Marine training to keep hold of his weapon. Or, in this case, a bottle of wine.

Footsteps ran into the kitchen. "Daddy, she's here. She's getting out of the car."

"I heard you."

"Shouldn't you be at the front door to say hi?"

"What I should do is be here to make the salad."

Her eyebrows lowered in disapproval. She was tightly coiled, ready to let go and spring up high. A lot of frustration in one small package. One twelve-year-old who was obviously playing matchmaker.

It made him want to laugh.

It made him happy.

The doorbell rang. Tori glared at him. "*I'll* get it." She spun around and ran out of the kitchen.

A second later, he heard the front door open. Setting the dinner plates on the table, he heard voices out in the hall, and he lifted his head and frowned. Was that a *male* voice?

Frowning harder, he left the plates and strode down the hall. Definitely a male voice. Now Tori was speaking again. And then a woman's voice, her enunciation clear and precise. Lauren.

He spotted Tori first at the end of the hallway. Across from her, Lauren stood in her gray coat. On Lauren's other side, near the front door, he could see jeans and a tuft of brown hair, the rest blocked by his daughter.

A man? Why would Lauren bring a man with her?

Tori was talking and waving her hands in the air, unfazed by the unexpected male. Then Tori's hands dropped to her sides, and she was leaning toward the man and listening.

Adam widened his stride as he headed toward them, ready to assess the situation.

Lauren's eyebrows arched up. Smiling almost shyly, she stepped toward him. And that's when he saw the man behind her, was not a grown man. It was the Fuller kid from next door, bending to pet Falco.

His muscles relaxed, and he laughed under his breath, though Josh was fourteen. Not exactly a kid anymore but close enough.

"I brought wine." Lauren lifted the bottle to show the label. The local winery. The same wine was in his refrigerator.

He thanked her and took it, then turned to Josh, asking how he was doing.

"Good." Josh straightened, and Falco remained at his side. If Adam had been a sentimental guy, he'd think that just because the dog liked Josh, that must mean he was okay.

But when it came to his daughter, Adam didn't go by sentiment. Josh seemed okay, but Adam remembered what he was like at fourteen. Not that he'd done anything with girls. But he'd wanted to. Wanted to badly.

"Josh's mom is working tonight," Tori said. "He brought over the hammer you loaned him." She held up the hammer. "Can he stay for dinner?"

"That's okay, Mr. Donahue. I'll be fine." Josh's face reddened. "I'm old enough to feed myself."

"We've got plenty of food," Adam said. Josh and his mom had moved into the house on his left last summer. Adam had lent Josh a few tools already and had helped him out a few times. Josh's mom worked the late shift at her uncle's gas station/mini-mart that was open year round. Before this, Josh and his mom had lived with Josh's grandmother, who'd finally sold her farm to live with her sister in Virginia. Before she'd left, she'd told everyone that Josh didn't need a babysitter anymore.

Maybe she was right. Maybe Josh didn't need a sitter. But everyone needed someone to be there some of the time. From what Adam could see, Diane—Josh's mom—didn't always come home right away after her shift was over. A couple of other neighbors had noticed that some nights she didn't come home at all.

"My mom doesn't want me to bother anyone about my dinner. I can make my own food." Josh scratched Falco's neck. "This is a cool dog."

"What are you making for your supper?" Adam asked.

"Um. Pizza."

Adam frowned. Frozen pizza probably. He shouldn't blame Diane. Being a parent was tough. Being a single parent was tougher. But being a kid was tough, too, and even at the old age of fourteen, a kid needed a parent who was there for him or her as much as possible.

"I'm making something a little better than that. It'll be done in about ten minutes. Stay and join us."

Josh's face flushed. "You don't have to do it."

"It's fine. We have plenty of food." He should've paid more attention to Josh. He'd noticed that the kid was on his own too often. It was none of his business, but at the least, he could've watched over him. Let him know that if he needed anything, he could call or come over.

He had his own problems, but that was no excuse. If Noelle were alive, she would say he was becoming a self-absorbed asshole, and he needed to snap out of it.

"Falco likes you, Josh," Tori said, her voice higher than usual. "You should stay."

Adam held back another groan. Falco wasn't the only one who liked the boy.

His daughter was too young for this.

He was too young for this.

He turned and stomped back toward the kitchen. He heard footsteps behind him and looked back. Lauren. She was carrying the hammer, and her closed lips were curved up in amusement.

He'd be amused, too, if it happened to a friend's daughter. But not *his* daughter. He'd been hoping to keep Tori a kid for another two or three years. Until she graduated from high school would have been about right, though he was pretty sure that wasn't going to happen. Not with her mom's smile and nose and her pretty hazel eyes.

"You're a good man." Lauren set the hammer on the counter where it would be out of the way. "Inviting Josh over for dinner. Taking care of your daughter."

"It's my *pleasure* to take care of her. What kind of father wouldn't do it?"

"Many." Her head tilted back, she sniffed the air. "Lasagna?"

"Spaghetti and meatballs." He opened the fridge to take out the big salad bowl and the small carafe of homemade salad dressing. "And salad."

"I'll help set the table." She headed to the right cabinet for the salad dishes, which he'd forgotten. He and Tori had gotten into the habit of using the dinner dish for salad. That way he didn't have to wash extra plates.

He set the dressing and the bowl of already mixed salad on the counter. "You remember where everything is?"

Kneeling to grab the salad plates from the lower cabinet, she glanced up at him, a smile softening the sharpness of her features. "It reminds me of when Noelle and I were teenagers.

When her mother worked, and Noelle did most of the cooking for the family. We spent a lot of time in that kitchen. I learned how to cook from her. You probably don't remember, but when you and she moved here, I helped her set up the kitchen. It's almost the same as her mom's."

"I didn't know that."

She flowed up to her feet. "It's a good memory."

This is a good memory, he thought but didn't say. He felt...at peace. Even though he knew there was no peace. Not a lasting one. There was his daughter with diabetes and no mother. Him with no wife. Josh next door with no supervision, and his daughter obviously had a crush on him.

To top it off, he had a mythological pooka—the feline version—napping in his daughter's bedroom.

He grimaced. He wasn't the only one with problems. "The word's out that you're looking for your husband's whereabouts. Any news?"

She carried the salad plates and an extra dinner plate for Josh to the table. He waited for her to set the plates out, then the silverware, with the napkins folded neatly. She worked quickly, and it almost seemed like a dance as she moved around so gracefully.

The last napkin in place, she looked up at him. "Nothing. I didn't expect to. That would be too easy."

He nodded. She'd told him that she was going make an effort to locate Paul and divorce him, so it shouldn't have been a surprise. But it was a jolt anyway. Things were changing

"So people are talking already," she said.

"Susie Meyers is. She works at the country club he went to."

"That was a good idea of my lawyer's. Paul loved his club. I think it made him feel manly."

He snorted. That said a lot about Paul. "You think he's alive?"

"I don't know for sure." She remained on the other side of the table. "I know he didn't love me. I don't think he had much love in his heart for anyone except himself. He did have some affection for his son. But both Wendy—his ex-wife—and I agree that Paul would never have disappeared without emptying his bank account and taking with him every asset that he could."

"You don't think he just snapped?"

"You knew Paul. Did he seem like the snapping kind to you?" She smiled, but it was the crookedest, saddest smile he'd seen.

It twisted something inside of him, something that made him step around the counter. "You shouldn't be alone tonight." Emotion heated inside him. Anger for Paul. Sorrow for her. Hunger for himself. "Stay here. You and Falco should stay here tonight."

Her breath sucked in, her eyes widening. For a few seconds, there was just him and her in the house. No one else.

"Let me make up for last time," he said, his voice so low that it croaked. "You can count on me."

"I'll be okay. I've been alone a long time." She gave him that twisted smile again. "Long before Paul left, I was alone."

He stared at her, and she stepped back,

putting distance between them. He wanted to say something. Noelle had talked about Lauren's parents. Unlike Josh's mother, her parents had been there for her physically, but emotionally they in some ways resembled an ice cube tray. She was so alone and so...beautiful...like a princess.

Since the first time he'd seen her, he'd liked the way she looked. But back then, he'd had Noelle. He and Noelle had been alike. Their parents had been working class. Lauren and her parents had been high class.

Yet she'd been Noelle's best friend.

Noelle had been gone for three years now.

And ten days ago, he'd kissed Lauren.

And she'd kissed him back.

And then he'd dropped her on the floor.

"I can't force you to stay here," he said, "but I'd feel better if you weren't alone."

"I'm not alone. I have Falco." She turned away, discussion over.

He stepped back. He had to respect her decisions. If he were honest, his reasons for wanting her to stay with them weren't pure.

His mom used to say that, at heart, all men were horn dogs. His mom had always been a smart woman.

Thirteen

Nothing new today. I'm napping.
~Pooka

"What exactly did your husband's associate say?" Adam asked.

Instead of answering, Lauren picked up her glass of wine—only the second for the night. Up to now, she'd been enjoying the evening. But Josh had gone home, and Tori had run upstairs to get ready for bed.

Lauren glanced at the star-shaped clock on the living room wall. A few minutes after ten already. It had been an odd night. Just conversation and laughter, and that bit of nervousness on her side. The same nervousness she'd had when she was a teenager and a cute boy was near.

She'd never known what to say to them. They'd never known what to say to her, either. She was tall and angular and self-conscious. If that wasn't enough, she was pedantic and didn't have a good sense of humor. Her parents were so serious, too.

If she'd dated someone like Adam, they would've hated it.

They'd liked Paul. When she'd mentioned his coldness to her mother, she'd looked at her blankly. Coldly.

She realized now that she'd married her parents.

Her hand shook slightly. Her parents might know by now that she was going to divorce Paul. Though they'd retired to Florida, where they resided in a condo by a golf course, they still had friends in the Door County area. The kind of friends who loved to gossip.

To be truthful, almost *everyone* she knew loved to gossip.

She stood. Falco, sprawled out in the corner, shifted his feet under him to stand.

Adam moved a step closer, too, only inches away.

Her skin prickled. "We should leave. Thank you for the lovely—"

He put his hand on her shoulder, stopping her words, staring into her eyes. "Don't be polite," he murmured.

Her legs felt buttery. Weak. And she prided herself on being a strong woman.

"What are we doing here?" She heard the breathlessness in her voice.

"I think we both know what we're doing. I'm attracted to you. I admire you. You make me laugh." His voice lowered. "You make me feel alive."

She bit her lower lip. She'd been attracted to him since she was seventeen. Eighteen years now. Her best friend's husband.

The odd thing was that she could have sworn she heard her old friend's laughter. Felt her approval, like warm sunlight on her shoulders.

Maybe it was the wine. Or maybe something empty and starving and needy inside her was pushing at her, shoving, working hard to pop out of her. A rebirth. It sounded impossible and crazy, but it wasn't like her to open her mouth and let words spew out.

Yet her mouth opened again. "It's, uh, mutual."

Immediately, she wanted to slap herself. *Mutual?* How unromantic could she be?

If she were going to say something, couldn't she do better than that?

He chuckled. "I love the way you say things."

She sighed, then reached her hand up, her palm and long fingers cupping the left side of his face. He leaned an increment into her palm and fingers. Like a baby who wanted more.

She wanted more, too. But was it safe?

Was anything safe?

She glanced over at Falco. He'd already settled down again, dozing on the rug. Falco was safe. She could trust him.

"It might be amusing to you now," she said, turning back to Adam. "*Now* is when you want to sleep with me."

The skin around his eyes crinkled into smile lines. "I hope there won't be a lot of sleeping involved."

Her face heated, and she was sure her cheeks were turning pink as he chuckled. She closed her eyes, sucked her breath in, then exhaled and opened her eyes. Straightening her spine, she looked into his eyes.

It was time to take a chance. It was past that time.

"Yes," she said. "Yes."

He closed in on her, his arms slipped around her back, his front solidly against hers. Not needing to ask what *yes* meant.

A moan came out of her mouth. They hadn't even kissed and she was turned on.

Only Adam. It had always been only Adam.

Their mouths met in a kiss that started hot and needy—and then it got hotter. Needier. As if all those years and all the nights she'd thought about him and imagined this embrace and this kiss were encapsulated into this one moment. All the nights she'd felt guilty because he was her best friend's boyfriend, then lover, then fiancée, then husband, then father of her child.

But Lauren had never been able to stop imagining this. Not even when she was married, and she and Paul had their regular Sunday morning exercise. Which was exactly what Paul used to call it: *Let's exercise now.*

She squirmed closer to Adam, loving the hard length pressing against her belly. She would love that length even better inside her body instead of outside.

And no more guilt. If her best friend was watching, Lauren knew exactly what Noelle would be doing right now: cheering them on.

He drew back. "We can't do it here."

"Where?"

"My office in the back."

"Okay." She started to turn, and he tugged her back.

"Another kiss first."

As he bent, she held back a cry. Forget the kiss. She wanted more. Much more. She wanted it all.

Then their lips were together and she was clinging to him again, on fire again. Wanting more and more and even more than that. She had never wanted a man as much as him.

He pulled away first, just looking at her, his eyes eating her face, drinking it in, as if memorizing every feature.

"Are you going to stop torturing me?" she asked.

"Oh, yes." He stepped back, and she could see in the brightness of his eyes that he was fully alive. Fully here. Fully into her the same way she was fully alive, fully here, and fully into him. He took her hand, gazing at her intently, and her breath sucked in.

For this moment, it wasn't just a man and woman who wanted sex. She couldn't say what it was. Just that it meant more. It went deeper. They were too good of friends and had too much of a history to take this next step lightly.

He took the step first. When she didn't immediately follow, he paused and looked back at her. Before he could say anything, she stepped up to his side.

No way was she chickening out on this. She was tossing safe and dull out the window.

"Let's go." She wanted to smile at him, but she felt too intense. Too consumed by her need for him.

Not smiling, either, he said, "Yes." And his voice was rough. "Let's hurry."

Their hands held tightly, they started toward the hall—

The doorbell rang.

She closed her eyes.

Adam stood still. So did she.

There was a noise, though, the sound of breathing in the living room. Falco. On his feet. Ready to protect her and her friends.

She didn't want Falco to defend her. If they didn't answer the door, surely whoever it was would go away soon.

Upstairs, a door slammed open, then fast footsteps in the hall, and then two feet stomping down the stairs.

She and Adam released each other's hand and jumped a foot apart.

Her cheeks felt hot again.

"It's Josh!" Tori's face was animated, her eyes bright. She didn't even glance at them, which was a good thing, Lauren thought. They probably looked guilty as hell.

"I'll get it." Adam strode down the hall, closer to the door than Tori, who was tying the sash of her pink fleece robe over striped purple pajamas and fluffy turquoise slippers.

"How did you know it was him?" Lauren asked Tori.

"Pooka told me."

His hand on the door handle, Adam looked

behind her, his eyes startled. "So you ran downstairs?" His tone wasn't happy.

Tori glared at her dad. "I didn't know there was a law against it."

Not even thinking, just reacting, Lauren took her hand.

The doorbell rang again, and Adam opened the door. Falco stood behind Adam and to the side. Not in attack mode, but there in case Adam needed him.

"What's wrong?" Adam asked.

Josh stepped inside, the door closing behind him. He wore the same jeans as earlier, and a worn-looking brown leather jacket. He stared straight at Lauren.

"There was an explosion. A house burned down, and I think it was your house."

Fourteen

When there's a fire, put it out or stay far away. ~Pooka

Lauren stared at the young teen.

"I thought you'd want to know." Josh looked so earnest, his forehead creased, his hair tousled. "You live in one of the stand-alone condos, just outside Sturgeon Bay? Near the bay side?"

She nodded, a sense of dread growing in her belly. As if her stomach was free-falling.

"I was watching TV," he said, "and the news interrupted my show. They said there was an explosion in one of the condos. They didn't know if the owner was in it, but the place was destroyed in, like, ten minutes. By the time the fire trucks got there, it was too late to save it."

She continued to stare. Too stunned to talk.

"A gas leak?" Adam asked.

Josh turned to him, shaking his head. "The fire chief was talking to the reporters. The first thing he said was that the explosion wasn't a gas leak."

"How did he know?" Lauren asked.

"I don't know. The chief didn't say, but he was real positive about that. Maybe it was a bomb, and they found pieces of it."

"Was Lauren's name mentioned?" Adam asked.

Josh shook his head.

"If they didn't say Lauren's name," Tori said, still holding Lauren's hand, "how do you know it was her place?"

"I don't know for sure, but after the fire chief stopped talking, the camera turned to a reporter who said she was talking to the woman's neighbor. She lived in the house near the burnt one. She said the firefighters had made her leave her home in case it caught on fire, too. Then she said that she hoped the woman and her dog were okay. The reporter asked what kind of dog it was, and the neighbor said it was an Irish wolfhound." He looked straight at Lauren. "I'm pretty sure it has to be you."

Tori made a sound of pain, and Lauren realized she was gripping Tori's hand too tightly. She dropped it and turned to her.

"I'm sorry. I'm sorry. I'm—"

Adam put his hand on her shoulders, turned her to him, and took her in his arms, stopping her babbling. "It's okay," he said, his voice rough. "You're okay. You and Falco are fine."

She nodded, and over his shoulder, she saw Tori staring at her. She *knew*. Only twelve years old, and she knew what they felt for each other.

She glanced over at Josh, and he had that same look of knowing.

Closing her eyes, she wrapped her arms around Adam. What the hell. So she was hugging a man, and he was hugging her back. She hadn't broken any laws.

"I'm fine." Her voice cracked, and tears were gathering in her throat. "Everything in the house can be replaced. It's all just things. That's all."

She was shaking, even though she kept telling herself she was okay. She was alive. And so was Falco. Thank God!

But in her head, she heard Josh saying, *They said there was an explosion in one of the condos. They didn't know if the owner was in it, but the place was destroyed in, like, ten minutes.*

She closed her eyes tighter. She'd left a light on in the living room and the kitchen, with music playing. It was a habit she'd gotten from her mother, who often said people were more likely to rob a house with no lights on and no sounds.

What if robbery hadn't been the intent?

What if it had been murder?

She was cold. So cold. And all she could think of was that maybe the fire chief had been wrong, and there had been a gas leak. Because if he was right, someone had blown up her house on purpose. Which meant that someone had picked her house at random...or someone had thought she was in the house and had blown it up with the intent to kill her.

Fifteen

Safe is a matter of opinion.
~Pooka

"I don't think you should let anyone know where you are." Tori's voice was high and squeaky. "Not even the fire people or the police."

Adam stared at Tori over Lauren's shoulder. Both of Lauren's arms were flung around him, and she was trembling. Behind her, Tori's gaze was unwavering, as if she expected him to say something wise. Something that would keep them all safe.

But Josh looked from Lauren to him, then at both of them together.

And he averted his eyes.

He *knew*.

Adam glanced down at the top of Lauren's head. Her medium brown hair was silky, straight, and glossy. If the children weren't in the room, he would bury his nose in her hair and breathe her scent in. He would run his fingers through it. He would drop a kiss on the crown, then whisper that she would be all right. He would swear that he'd watch over her and wouldn't let anyone harm her. He would swear on his heart.

He closed his eyes instead, and as he did, she moved, pulling her arms away from him, standing straight and stiff.

His eyes opened. She smiled at him ruefully, her lips crooked. "I'll call the sheriff," she said. "I'll—"

"No," he said.

Her eyebrows shot up. "I have to talk to someone at the sheriff's office. They probably already know about my plans to divorce Paul. Too many people do. At the hospital today, I saw Paul's associate. He mentioned it. I'm sure he's not the only one."

Tori's forehead scrunched. "What's an associate?"

Lauren turned to her. "After my husband started his insurance agency, he wanted it to grow, and he took Darryl in to work with him."

"Was your husband his boss?" Josh asked.

"Kind of," Lauren said. "Darryl was building his own client list, and now he takes care of Paul's clients, too."

"He gets extra for that?"

"Of course."

"He's an insurance agent," Adam said. "They don't give anything away."

"You still get money?" Tori asked her.

"A smaller amount, though Darryl is recompensed for taking care of the accounts. But I don't keep it. I'm giving it to Paul's son."

"If Darryl's taking care of the accounts," Tori said, "that doesn't seem fair."

"Actually, it is fair. Paul started the agency, put his money into it, and built a reputation that..." She paused and looked at Adam.

He raised his eyebrows but didn't reply. This part wasn't anything to do with him.

"Anyway"—she turned back to Tori—"he's not the only one who was contacted by my lawyer's investigator."

"Maybe he killed your husband!" Tori did a short jump, her hands clapped together. "And now it's your turn."

"Darryl was with clients all day at the time of Paul's disappearance. I was questioned extensively, and he was, too. One of the deputies let it slip to me. So, no, it's not possible." She frowned. "And if you saw him... He's not athletic. I think he'd have problems killing a squirrel."

"You don't have to be athletic to kill," Josh said. "Not if you have a gun."

She looked at Adam again. He saw the questions in her face. The sadness.

He remembered her eyes at Noelle's funeral. She'd been so composed, but her eyes were red. *If I can do anything,* she'd said, *call me. I'll be there.*

Instead of taking her up on it, he'd resented her help the one time she'd given it. He'd been stupid. He'd been mourning. Maybe it was just as well. She'd had her own life, her own problems. She hadn't asked him for help, and he'd learned to take care of his own life. Just him and Tori and the awful, gaping hole in their lives.

Now Lauren was the one who needed him, and he wasn't going to stay out of her life. Noelle

would want him to be here for her. So would Tori.
He wanted to be here for her.

"What if your husband is still alive?" Josh asked. "What if he found out about that you're getting ready to divorce him? Like you said, everyone around here has heard about it. Even I heard about it. Do you think he'd blow up your house?"

She stilled, and so did Adam.

"I can't imagine..." Her voice was so low he had to lean forward to hear her. "Most of the time I think he's dead."

"Doesn't the sheriff think he was probably drowned or something?" Tori asked. "That's what I heard."

"You two are asking a lot of questions." Adam gave his daughter the stern look that said she was about to step over the line.

"If we don't ask questions, we won't get any answers." She glanced over at Josh. "Isn't that right?"

Josh grinned, and Tori turned her gaze back to him and Lauren. "Besides, Josh and I care about Lauren. She's my *godmother.* I have to watch out for her. Right?"

Lauren stepped forward, then bent to hug Tori. He could see Lauren's slim, tense back, and he pictured her fierce expression and the way she scrunched her face as she tried not to cry.

"We don't know if he's alive or dead," Adam said. "His body was never found."

Lauren pushed away from Tori. Adam put his hand on Lauren's shoulder, letting her know she wasn't alone.

"You think he's drowned, don't you?" As Tori spoke, she looked from Lauren to him, then back to Lauren.

He stiffened and removed his hand from Lauren's shoulder. This was awkward. He'd explain to Tori tomorrow how he felt about Lauren. That they were friends...and that maybe they were on their way to becoming better friends.

Maybe he would tell her. After all, he didn't know what Lauren thought. Or felt.

He only knew what he felt, but he wasn't sure what he wanted to do. This was happening so fast, and he'd never been a fast guy. Not that way.

And now her house had been blown up.

"The deputies never found his body, did they?" Josh asked. "All I heard is that they just found his abandoned car. Maybe he's hanging around someplace. Maybe he's the one who planted the explosives."

"Don't believe everything you hear," Adam said, and he put his hand back on Lauren's shoulder.

"Just what we see." Tori looked from his face to his hand on Lauren's shoulder and back to his face.

Lauren twisted to look into his eyes. "We should leave this to the sheriff's office."

"I agree," Adam said.

"I'll talk to them..." She stopped, her shoulders sloping down, and when she spoke, her voice was tired. "I should call them now."

Tori shivered. "The whole thing sounds creepy to me."

"Creepy is the perfect word." Lauren tried to smile at Tori, but her lips trembled.

In that moment, Adam had a sense that she'd felt alone for so long. And now, she was...less alone. And the feeling was overpowering her. He didn't know where that thought came from, but—

Meeee, a catlike voice said inside Adam's head. *Meeee*.

Adam shook his head. This was a bad time to imagine that the pooka was talking to him. "When you call," Adam said to Lauren, "say that you're staying with me. And tell them *not* to tell anyone."

"Adam, I can't stay here." Lauren took a step back. "I can't put Tori in danger. This might be the next house that blows up."

Tori cried out, a wordless protest, and Lauren swung back to face her.

Adam stared at Lauren. Not wanting to consider her words as truth.

But he had to. He had to think of his daughter. He even had to think of Josh.

"I mean it." Lauren kept her gaze on Tori, her normally clear voice husky with sadness. "Your mother was my best friend, and you're my goddaughter, and your father and I... We're friends, too. If something happened to any of you because I was here..."

"You'd kill yourself." Tori put her hand over her breast. "Like one of the heroines in a Shakespeare play?"

"*No*! I'd—" Lauren stopped talking, her back slumped, her neck curved, and her chin down. A posture of surrender.

Adam closed his eyes and let go of his tension. She'd given up. She couldn't even finish the sentence. She'd fought hard, but she wasn't going to fight anymore.

This was insight into her way of thinking. When you didn't fight, you didn't lose. Common sense had won the day, and maybe she was right. Maybe if they stood back and let the authorities take care of it, everything was going to be okay. Somehow, someway, it was going to be okay.

Only he couldn't believe it. There had to be something he could—

A thought popped into his mind. He glanced upward, then toward his daughter. "Why don't you go upstairs and ask the pooka her opinion? Just you and Lauren."

Tori's smile faded. "Dad, only I can see and talk to Pooka. I don't think she wants to talk to anyone but me."

Adam glanced at Josh, who watched Tori, his expression alert but not puzzled. *He knew.* Tori must have told him about the pooka.

"The pooka is Tori's, um, friend," Lauren said. "No one else's. I don't need to be there. I understand just how she feels."

"You do?" Tori stared at her.

Lauren nodded decisively. "Yes. She's your special friend, and you don't want to share her. That's fine with me. I know you'll talk to her and say all the right things."

Tori stared for another moment, frowning. Adam had never thought of himself as sensitive, but he felt the tension in the air. He gazed at Josh, who stood silently with his eyes flickering from Tori's face to Lauren's and then back to Tori again. Not saying a word.

Smart kid. Adam was twenty-three years older than Josh, and he kept his mouth shut, too.

"I'd like you to go upstairs with me." Tori held out her hand to Lauren. "Let's go now."

Lauren took Tori's hand, her eyes widening.

"Josh and I will stay down here," Adam said.

"Yeah." Josh nodded. "We'll wait here."

"Falco, too." Adam put his hand on Falco's neck over his collar. "We'll let it be an all-girl conversation."

Tori giggled, then sobered quickly as she and Lauren headed toward the stairs. Neither female looked back or replied. They just started up the stairs, Tori rushing ahead while Lauren marched up behind her as he and Josh watched them.

There were only two of them, and one was only twelve, but it seemed to Adam that he was looking at an army.

Sixteen

Humans don't understand that what they do today—right now—is what forms their future. ~Pooka

Tori reached the upstairs hallway five steps ahead of Lauren. Lauren's complexion was paler than usual, but Tori was pretty sure hers was pinker. She felt pink today, as pink as her robe, the blood thrumming through her veins and into her face.

This was turning into the most exciting year ever. And the scariest. Well, since her mom had been gone.

The thought brought up the usual lump in her throat. Then Lauren stepped up in the hall and curved her hand over her shoulder, and the lump shrunk and she breathed easier.

"Take me to the pooka," Lauren said, pushing Tori in front of her.

Tori giggled, because it sounded funny. But just before they reached the door, she stopped and looked behind her at Lauren, who raised one eyebrow in a question.

"I was thinking about my mom. I wish she were here." Even as the last word came out of her mouth, Tori stiffened. She knew what Lauren would say. That her mom wouldn't want her to mourn forever. That her mom would want her to go on with her life. That her mom would want her to fill her life up with good things and good people. And blah blah blah blah blah.

Her eyes heated and stung, and she blinked furiously to keep the tears from leaking out.

"Don't you ever think," Lauren said, her voice as level as her gaze, "that she's with you right now?"

Tori stared, feeling her eyes widen, the tears drying.

"Why do you think the pooka came to you?" Lauren put her hands on her hips. "Do you think pookas go to every girl?"

Tori's mouth dropped open. "You think my mom sent Pooka to me?"

"I don't know, but she used to love unicorns, even when she was a teenager. She would draw them on her papers during class. I bet she would love a pooka."

The tears started again, but a smile was growing on Tori's face, bigger by the second until she couldn't talk anymore. Just smiled like the boy in school who had something wrong with him. He didn't talk. He just smiled. Some of the other kids made fun of him, but she always smiled back at him.

Now she thought she would smile back at him longer and bigger. Maybe he had a pooka, too, that spoke only to him. Maybe that's why he smiled. Maybe she would even talk to him.

"Let's go." Lauren took her hand.

Still smiling and her eyes still watery, Tori took her into her room. And there was Pooka on her bed, licking a paw. As if she were cleaning herself up, getting ready for company.

Tori looked up at Lauren. "Can you see her?"

Lauren shook her head. Tori turned to Pooka. "You can let Lauren see you. She won't hurt you."

"No human can hurt me. And it's better that no one but you can see me."

"Better for what? And I only told my dad, Josh, and Lauren."

"Tell one person, you may as well tell the world."

"They won't tell anyone. I promise!"

"That's what you think." Pooka's voice was languid. *"I've had that said to me before, and I've been disappointed before."*

"You're very distrustful."

"No, I'm realistic. But never mind. You see what you want to see."

Tori whipped her gaze up to Lauren, who was watching her with a slight frown on her forehead.

"Can you hear her?" Tori asked.

Lauren shook her head. "I can see and hear you, but it feels like there's a ripple in the air." She held out her hand above Pooka's head that was craned upward, watching every move she made.

"You're close," Tori said. "About another inch down."

Pooka sniffed. Lauren's hand lowered.

"If she pets me, she's going to get claw marks across the back of her hand."

Tori grabbed Lauren's wrist. "She doesn't want you to pet her."

"Okay. I won't try to touch her."

Tori let go, and Lauren's arm dropped to her side. "Is it all right for me to ask her a question?" Lauren asked.

"She can ask. I might or might not answer."

Tori swallowed a giggle. "Yes."

Lauren bent her knees, looking down to where the pooka would be if she were a regular cat. Tori bit her lower lip to keep from telling her that she was looking at the pooka's chest and front feet. Pooka wouldn't care. If she did, she'd show herself. And though it was hard to read Pooka's face, Tori was pretty sure she was amused instead of insulted.

"Have you met Noelle?" Lauren asked. "Tori's mom? Did Noelle send you here?"

Tori sucked in her breath. These questions had been in her mind, but she'd been afraid to ask. She'd been afraid of the answer.

"I don't know."

Tori shook her head, then closed her eyes. Her face scrunched. Lauren made a crooning sound of sympathy, then stood and pulled her against her so that Tori's head rested on her chest.

"It's okay." Lauren patted her back. "Your mom is watching you. Loving you and your dad. I know this."

Tori lifted her head from Lauren's small breast, not caring that Lauren saw tears in her eyes. "How do you know this for sure?"

"Because I'm here. Don't you think that your mom sent me here?"

"So we can help you?"

Lauren nodded. "And maybe so I can help you and your dad."

A hiss came from the pooka, and Tori turned her head toward her.

"*It could be possible I was sent here by your mother's request.*"

"You mean..." Tori gulped and stared at her. "Do you mean," Tori said again, "that my mom put this request in to *God*?"

"*I can't answer that.*"

"You can't because it's against the rules? Or you can't because you don't know?"

"*Maybe both. All I can tell you is one thing.*" Pooka paused, as if for a dramatic moment.

"What thing is that?" Tori asked, aware of Lauren's gaze on her.

The pooka stared into her eyes. "*It's that there's only one real answer to every question. Only one real thing.*"

"What real thing?" Tori whispered. "Tell me."

Pooka bumped her forehead against Tori's arm, then pulled back. "*It's that only one thing matters most in life.*"

"Is it..." The word stuck in her mouth, but she spat it out. "Love?"

"*What do you think?*" Pooka curled up on the bed again, lowering her head onto the soft, puffy cover. "*I'm going to sleep now. You can go away.*"

Tori looked up at Lauren, her mouth hanging open.

"What did the pooka say?" Lauren asked.

Tori just shook her head. She wasn't sure what Pooka meant. Wasn't sure if she meant love. Or if she meant chocolate. Or maybe even meant taking a nap in a circle of sunlight, since that seemed to be Pooka's favorite thing to do.

Tori was only twelve! She knew a lot for her age. More than most kids, because she'd been through so much. But she didn't know *everything*.

If the answer really was love, why was there so much hatred in the world? Why were people killing each other?

Why did people drink too much, then get into their cars and run people over?

Or why did people just disappear, like Lauren's husband?

"Nothing," Tori said. "The pooka said nothing."

Even if it were love, she wasn't sure if she believed it. She wasn't sure of anything—except one. That most people didn't care about most other people.

And the people who cared about you...they might die.

She knew about dying. Knew that it didn't just happen to other people, like most kids her age thought. It happened to people she loved. And if she didn't take care of herself, it could happen to her.

Seventeen

People only believe what you say when they want to believe what you say.
~Pooka

At the bottom of the staircase, it hit Lauren that this was real. That her house had burnt down. That there'd been an explosion, and it probably wasn't a gas leak, which could mean... Insanity, that's what it could mean. That someone might have tried to kill her. Though right now, it was only a possibility. Not a reality. She'd sooner believe in the pooka than believe that someone had tried to kill her.

Gripping the railing knob, she stepped down and stood in the hall, catching her composure. Trying not to look as if she were about to throw up any second. Tori had stayed upstairs, primping in the bathroom. For Josh, Lauren suspected, and that thought didn't make her feel better.

"How'd it go?" Josh asked from the couch in the living room. "Did the pooka let you see it?"

She shook her head, not able to speak yet. If she did, she didn't know what would come out. A cry. A scream. Crazy laughter.

She forced her hand to open up and let go of the knob, then she stepped carefully into the living room. She'd been humoring Tori in her bedroom, but at the same time, it had felt as if a pooka really was curled up on the bed. A giant invisible cat that talked.

Maybe she just wanted to believe that in her practical, fact-ordered, day-by-day existence—at least before today—a whimsical, giant cat existed.

She glanced first at Josh, on the couch, frowning at his phone. Then Adam, who sat on the couch with his legs wide apart, the way men often did.

A cell phone buzzed. Adam grabbed his phone from the table next to him, looked at the display, then set it down again. "A client. I'll call him back later."

"I hadn't even thought of my purse." She hurried to her purse on the table by the coat closet. "I turned my phone off before I came over. I didn't want to—" She clamped her lips together, but the thought in her mind carried through. *Be bothered by anyone while I was with you and Tori.*

She fished out her phone from her purse and turned it on. The messages were all there. As she looked at them, her hand started to wobble.

People probably thought she was dead.

Glancing through, she saw five from her mother and three from her father.

Of course they'd heard. Even in Florida, they

still kept in touch with a few of the orchestra musicians.

Three messages were from the sheriff's department.

Two from Ashleigh at work—

A hand curved over her shoulder, steadying her. Only then did she realize her whole body was shaking. She twisted her neck to look up at Adam's face.

"Turn it off," he said.

She still stared at him.

"We don't want anyone to know where you are."

"Because of Tori?" She didn't blame him. Though they didn't know if someone had tried to kill her, of course he wouldn't want to put Tori in any possible danger.

"I was thinking of you, but Tori, too."

"And you."

"I wasn't thinking of myself." His voice was low. Brusque.

"Once a Marine, always a Marine?" She kept her voice light, aware of Josh watching them. Aware of footsteps upstairs, then Tori running down the hallway, her steps light. Different from Lauren's heart that was beating so hard.

She stepped away from Adam. "I have to call my mother." Though her mother and father weren't warm and fuzzy, they cared for her in their own way. They were very...responsible. She was their only child, and they had taken care of her and had done the best they could, given their limited emotions. They needed to know she was alive.

"If you ask them not to tell anyone, will they keep quiet?"

She nodded. "I'll make it clear that if they mentioned it to anyone, there could be consequences."

"They'd understand that?" he asked.

"Someone burned down my house today. My parents are very intelligent. They'll understand."

Before she could say any more, Tori jumped the last two steps to land on the hall floor, then glanced over at Josh. Making sure he noticed her.

Uh oh. Lauren winced. Nothing else, because maybe there was nothing else but just *uh oh.*

She grabbed her phone, then headed to the kitchen to talk to her parents privately. Her mother answered quickly, her voice brusque and shaky. Maybe it was the connection, but Lauren had the feeling that she'd been crying.

She set those speculative and probably incorrect thoughts aside. If she mentioned her assumptions to her mother, she would embarrass both of them. It was better to pretend she didn't hear the worry.

Lauren told her mother she was staying at a friend's house over the evening. She would call the sheriff's the next morning. She added that she hoped her mother wouldn't mention that she was alive.

"I won't say anything," he mother said, her usual smooth tone back. "Except, of course, to your father."

"Of course," Lauren said. Her father would never discuss her with their friends, so that wasn't a worry. He only discussed subjects that interested him. Her mother, though an intellectual, too, at least had a practical streak. She'd been the one to sign all of Lauren's report cards. The one who went to teacher's conferences. The one who'd paid for extracurricular activities and school fees, and who had attended a couple of debates in which Lauren had participated in high school. She'd even brought Lauren's father with her exactly three times. Lauren remembered each one. Though she didn't know what promises her mother had made to him to get him to the debates, she'd appreciated her mother's efforts.

"Where exactly are you staying?" her mother asked.

Not answering, Lauren stood still.

"Adam Donahue's house, right?"

Lauren winced, annoyed at herself for mentioning her recent connection with Adam and his daughter in their last weekly phone call. She knew how incredibly smart her mother was. When it came to her pickup on things like this, she was the Einstein of Door County. Although now it was her Florida community.

"We are friends," Lauren said.

There was a moment of silence as Lauren clenched the muscles in her body. She opened her mouth to say good-bye when her mother said, "I have to admit that, if I had to trust any man to take care of you, it would be Adam."

Lauren's mouth stayed open.

"I believe now that your father and I were wrong about Paul. Very wrong."

"Um, well..." Lauren sucked in her breath. "In

the end, it was my decision, not yours. I'd better go now. I'll call you tomorrow night."

She hung up and turned around, feeling light-headed.

This was the strangest day in her life. She'd lost her house. She'd lost her things.

But it felt like she was gaining something else. Pieces of herself that she'd been dropping for years were coming back to her, like eggshells flying back to the egg.

She straightened her shoulders and walked back to the living room. So awkward. So odd. So sad. So scary.

And so *alive*.

Eighteen

True and False cannot live together peacefully. It's a law of nature. ~Pooka

Josh muttered that he had to get to bed. Tori watched him leave, and Adam could see the yearning in her gaze.

He winced. At the end of summer, she'd had the same yearning look when they drove by the ice cream shop.

His little girl had graduated from ice cream to boys.

Then Lauren stepped up to her side, and Tori's eyes sparkled. They didn't look alike, but in spirit they had too much in common. They'd been bruised. Lauren by the coldness of her parents— and perhaps her husband, too. Tori by her diabetes and her mother's death.

Adam had tried to make up for it, but he couldn't be everything to her, and he couldn't do everything for her. He could only do the best he could. The hell of it was that his best never seemed to be good enough.

It hurt Adam to see Tori hanging on Lauren now. At the same time, it made him feel as if everything was going to be okay.

It wasn't that Lauren was like Noelle. They'd always been opposites, and maybe their differences had made them friends. Maybe that's why Tori accepted Lauren so easily. Lauren treated Tori as an adult, too, speaking to her as if they were equals. Even when Tori was a baby and then a toddler, Lauren had talked to Tori as a smaller adult. It used to make him smile.

It made him smile now, too, though he still hurt. As if he were letting go of something he loved.

Noelle. His wife. The mother of his child. His first love. The woman he still loved. The woman he would always love.

But he looked at Lauren, and the blood rushed inside him faster and stronger.

And hotter.

His heart hammered.

Feelings that had been slugging along on low power for the last three years were alive now. Brilliantly, full-steam-ahead alive. Maybe too alive and too fast. Like a runaway train, and he wanted to run all over her.

It was a good thing that Tori was in the room...

A wordless yawn came from Tori, and he switched his gaze to her, her mouth wide open. No polite putting her hand over her mouth. And why should she? She was safe here. With him, Lauren, Falco, and maybe even the pooka, though he still was having a hard time with the pooka stuff. Right now, he didn't want to think about it.

"It's past your bedtime," he said.

Tori scowled, then opened her mouth again—no doubt to complain—when Lauren said, "I'm getting tired, too. This was a full day."

"I guess I still have to go to school tomorrow," Tori said.

"You bet you will." Adam spoke in his *I'm the big, bad giant* voice that he'd used to read fairy tales to Tori when she was young.

Tori giggled. "Okay, but when I'm in bed, can Lauren come and say good night?"

Adam felt a twist in his chest, and he could see by Lauren's stillness that she was surprised. It had been years since Tori had needed him to say good night at her bedside.

"Call out when you're ready," Lauren said. "I'll be up there."

Tori beamed, then rushed upstairs, her slippers making flopping noises on each step.

Lauren turned to him. "I hope you don't mind."

"No." He stood. "You want anything to drink? I have wine and beer."

"I'm okay. I really am tired. It's been a full day."

"You can sleep in my bed. I'll—"

"Absolutely not. Do you still have the pullout couch in the basement? I can sleep there. If I recall correctly, it was very comfortable."

He stared at her for a long moment. He remembered coming home from a hunting trip once, and she and Noelle were both ensconced on the pullout bed, eating popcorn and giggling. He'd grinned and had a couple dirty thoughts that he'd quickly banished.

An ache throbbed in his heart. Not a sad ache. A good one.

"If you insist." He stood. "I'll go upstairs and get covers."

Upstairs, he could hear Tori brushing her teeth. It almost seemed to him that her happiness beamed out of the bathroom, like sunlight. She was making Lauren's loss her gain.

He felt the same way, though that wasn't anything he wanted to think about. Especially since the explosion meant someone might have tried to kill her, and might try again.

Walking downstairs with the quilt, linens, and pillow, he was more sober than he'd been running up to the second floor. Lauren was on the couch in the living room. She got up, slowly, which was unlike her. She seemed different. Fragile.

"I'm ready!" Tori called from the upper floor.

He dumped the bedding on the chair nearest him as Lauren smiled crookedly at him. "It's a strange day," she said.

He watched her go upstairs, his gaze on the sway of her hips. Not a *look at me* sway, but just the natural movement of a woman's body.

After she disappeared, he realized she needed more than covers, and he headed upstairs, too, making a mental list. Toothbrush and toothpaste. He could lend her an old T-shirt, plus a pair of Christmas boxers his mom had given him about three years ago that he'd never worn but kept in his dresser in case his mom asked about them.

In his bedroom, he dug the items out. At the

last second, he grabbed the flannel red-and-navy-checked housecoat he rarely wore, either. Another gift from his mom.

He met Lauren coming out of Tori's bedroom, closing the door carefully so it would make a muted click. Her normally serious expression had softened, her lips parted instead of pressed together.

"I think she was tired," she murmured. "She fell asleep as I was talking to her."

He wanted to kiss her. Instead, he held out the boxers, T-shirt, and robe to her.

"For me?"

He nodded. He didn't seem to be good with words today. He'd never been loquacious, but the last time he'd been this tongue-tied had been with Noelle. He'd still been in his teens and was falling in love.

"Bedclothes," he said, then groaned inwardly. Who said *bedclothes*? "For going to bed," he added, then wanted to groan again. What had happened to his power to speak clearly? He tilted his chin toward the bathroom. "There's a new toothbrush you can use there." He stepped back. "This is a bad idea. You should sleep in my bed. I'll get my stuff and—"

"No." Her voice firm, she took the items from him. "You sleep in your own bed. I can sleep just fine in the basement. Besides"—she smiled—"it's probably a good idea to keep Falco away from the pooka. It is a cat, you know."

"A giant dog and a giant cat." He grimaced. "My house isn't that big. Good thing only one of them is real."

She started to chuckle—and the lights turned off and on three times over.

They both looked up at the ceiling and then at each other.

"Very...odd." She stepped back. "I'll change in the bathroom here before I go downstairs. Thanks."

"I'll take Falco out." As he turned away, he added, "And no arguments."

Soft chuckles followed him.

This had been a bad day for Lauren, and he shouldn't feel so good. But he did. Hormones. Damned inconvenient and stronger than his common sense. But after three years of sadness, there was something unusual happening inside him.

Horniness? Hell yes. He wasn't going to deny that.

But it was more. It was...something elusive. Something that made him feel fully awake, as if all the possibilities that had been shut to him three years ago were now glowing in front of him, waiting for him to walk to the invisible gates, push them open, and go for it.

He didn't know if he would.

All he knew as he ran down the stairs was that he sure the hell wanted to.

Nineteen

Sometimes humans are run by their hormones. As a pooka, I take advantage of that. As a cat, I don't give a damn.
~Pooka

Adam and Falco were waiting in the living room when Lauren came down. She wore his nightclothes and his housecoat while he was still in his jeans and sweatshirt. She dumped her clothes on the chair near the stairway.

"Thanks for this." Lauren plucked one of the flannel sleeves. Falco came to her side, and smooshed his big head against her arm.

"You like that, too," she murmured. She rubbed below his ears and his chin, smiling down at him.

Then she looked straight at Adam's face, and there was hunger in his eyes that stared at her as if he were starving. And not for food. Starving for softness. Kindness. And, to be honest—because she always tried to be honest with herself—sex.

Her body responded. But her mind... Thank

God her mind was still functioning, screaming at her to slow down. Slow way down.

"It's been a long day." Her voice wanted to soften, to thicken, to tremble, but she forced herself to speak succinctly. She forced herself to stand still instead of clasping her hands and wringing them, like a Victorian virgin heroine alone with a man.

She was no heroine. And she certainly was no virgin. And though sex could be pleasant, in her experience, the end result was often a disappointment. It was like going to a place famous for desserts and discovering that the dessert was just not that great.

Yet everyone else seemed to love the dessert. So she would go back a different time and order something else, her mouth watering because it looked so damn good.

And she would feel the same disappointment. Again.

And again.

And again.

Not any of them stood up to her homemade desserts that were just better.

Often, even the unhealthy ones from the box on the grocery store shelves were better, too.

She chuckled.

"What's funny?" he asked.

Hearing the husky thickness in his voice, she shivered. "I was thinking about desserts." And realizing she'd gone back for desserts at the supposedly wonderful dessert place more often than she'd gone back to men.

Certainly, sex with Paul had never been

wonderful. She'd married him for his suitability. For a child—which had never happened. She'd had herself tested, and she was fine. He had told her his sperm count was fine, too...

But she'd wondered. Doubted. Suspected.

Though he did have a son, he wasn't always there for Rodney. And he'd never been concerned that she didn't conceive. It could be possible that at some time—either before or after their marriage—he'd had a vasectomy.

A movement from her side caught her attention. Falco. His head tilted up at her, he opened his mouth and out came a long, mournful sound that ended with a few *woo woos*.

"Sweetheart." She bent to hug him, and he pushed his head against hers again. "It's okay," she murmured, rubbing the shaggy fur on his neck. "It's all okay."

"Falco's a great dog." Adam started toward her.

She kept one hand on Falco's head. "I should take him outside."

"Done already."

"Right. I forgot." With him so near, a foot away from her now, she was forgetting to breathe. This close, it felt as if his body were pulling her to him, like the sun's gravitational pull on the earth.

She shivered. Not because she was cold but because she thought that maybe this dessert she would like. Or even love.

Maybe she would love it too much.

The thought made her gulp, but she didn't back down. She stayed standing and straightened her spine and looked straight at him.

"What do you want?" she asked.

"Anything you want. Anything."

She stared into his eyes, the wonderful blue gaze that wouldn't leave hers. The face that was strong and caring and intense and still boyish. The face of the boy she'd fallen in love with when she was seventeen.

The boyfriend of her best friend. Now her best friend's widowed husband. The father of her goddaughter.

And she knew what she wanted.

Everything.

But he couldn't give her everything.

"I think I want the same thing." And to her ears, her voice had the same mournful note as Falco. "But would it..." She stopped, took a shaky breath. Holding her head high, she worked hard to keep her voice steady. "Would it *change* things?"

Her voice wobbled on *change*, and she wasn't thinking of the old, pre-pooka life change. She was thinking of this new relationship. This friendship. This...whatever it was.

When he didn't answer, she thought perhaps he hadn't heard her. After all, she'd been pretty sure that Paul hadn't heard three-fourths of what she'd said. He'd perfected his *uh huh* responses.

She stopped her thoughts, pushing Paul out of her mind. Keeping her attention on this man who'd been the love of her life, though he'd never known. This man who was frowning slightly, thinking over her question, and clearly sorting it out.

In that moment, she knew what she needed to say. This might be her one chance with Adam. If she didn't say yes, for the rest of her life she would wonder what she'd missed.

She would wonder about the kisses that she hadn't gotten.

The touches that she'd missed.

The skin sliding against skin...

She gulped back a moan.

"It always changes." He put his hand on the side of her face. "The choice is yours."

He was only touching her face, and she wanted to melt into a puddle of need.

"Not here," she said.

He pulled his hand back, and she felt the loss. Her skin where he'd touched it was cold, already missing the touch of his fingers. "The basement," he said. "The pullout couch from when..."

"When you and Noelle rented the duplex." She remembered sleeping on it when he was on a hunting trip with friends, and Noelle was pregnant and didn't want to be alone. Noelle had ended up sleeping with her. It had felt like they were young teens again at a sleepover. They'd giggled and laughed and eaten popcorn.

Every year after that during hunting season, they'd had a sleepover. Even when Noelle and Adam had moved into this house. Even when she'd been married to Paul.

At least Paul had never complained, though she knew the reason he'd never complained was that he'd never cared.

Adam shook his head. "Noelle and I never made love on—"

"Stop." She grabbed her clothes, tucked them

under her arm, then held out her other hand for his. "Let's go downstairs."

He grabbed the bedding and the pillow with his left hand, then took her hand in his right. As they started down the stairs, he closed the basement door behind her.

Her eyebrows rose in a question.

"He might get jealous," he said.

"He might bark," she said.

He laughed low in his throat, then they headed down the stairs. As she followed him, she noticed that her breathing was fast. And then they were in the basement, with all the walls paneled about four feet up, a leftover from the previous owners.

She knew all this, and it made her smile.

And there was the couch, covered in a sturdy brown-and-orange tweedy material. She shivered, then dumped her clothes on the stuffed chair in the corner. He draped the quilt over her shoulders, wrapping it like a shawl. She stood unmoving as he lowered his head, still holding on to the edges of the quilt.

Protecting her.

She closed her eyes as his lips touched hers.

Her lips opened a little, she sighed.

Then he let go of the quilt and his arms reached around her.

It felt like...coming home.

Maybe...just maybe...this would be better than homemade dessert.

Twenty

I don't know why humans think what they do during mating is special. It's the same thing every other animal does.
~Pooka

It was like butter.

Adam's grandmother used to say that, and he'd never known what it meant. Until now. The minute their lips met, it felt like it was meant to be.

He felt the tension sweep away from her, as if she were coming home in his arms.

And he...he felt like he'd been up at bat, and after a lot of foul balls and walks, he'd hit the ball out of the park. For the second time in his life.

All he had to do now was take it easy and enjoy.

She pulled back first. "The bed," she said, and her voice was breathy.

He wanted to holler out a victory yell, but there was no victory yet. Instead, he should be singing some sexy blues song, and if he'd planned ahead, he would've done it.

"What are you thinking?" She lifted her hand, turning it, sliding the backs of her long fingers down the side of his face.

"That I'm glad you're alive."

"I won't die on you. Not for a long time."

"Promise?" He heard the urgency in his voice.

She smiled, and the intensity in her face softened. "Yes," she murmured. "Yes."

"I'll pull out the couch."

"I'll help." She headed toward the couch at his side. He went to the far side. Working together, they pulled it out in less than a minute.

He quickly put one sheet on the bottom, then the quilt on the side, ready to tug over them. He gestured toward the pullout sofa, but she didn't get in right away.

Instead, she started to strip. He watched, his body heating and hardening as she stood on the other side of the bed, tall and on the slender side, but with the wonderful curve of her waist and her hips. Her chin was up, and so was one eyebrow and both corners of her lips.

"Did you see enough?" she asked, then laughed at him. As if, in shedding the shirt and Christmas boxers, she'd shed her inhibitions.

"I could look at you forever."

She put her hand on one of the gorgeous hips. "I hope not. It's chilly in here, and in a moment I'm going to be covered up with the quilt. But first, I'm hoping to see what I'm getting."

He laughed, a rumble of joy. "I've never seen you like this."

"Like what?"

"So..." He unbuttoned his jeans and noticed

her eyes following the movement of his fingers. "Playful."

She laughed. So did he. *Playful* was a word he was sure he'd never used before—and it had probably never been used to describe Lauren—but it fit her tonight.

"Today is a miracle," she said, no longer laughing but no sadness in her eyes, either. Just a brightness that had nothing to do with the industrial ceiling lights. "It dawned on me as we walked down the steps that if I hadn't been on the way to your place, I might be dead."

"So, I inadvertently saved your life."

"You and Tori. Now, are you taking your clothes off, or is there something you don't want me to see?"

Before she finished the last word, he was pushing down his jeans, hopping on one foot, then the other, the sock on his left foot coming off with the jeans, so he tore off the other sock, too. As if it were an afterthought, he pulled off his shirt and tossed that on the carpet.

Then he straightened, his chin up, holding his arms open on each side. His legs open, too, braced. Letting her have a good look. A good look at *everything.*

And she looked, taking her time, her half smile growing into a full smile.

"Will it do?" He grinned back at her.

She set one knee on the bed, then crooked her finger at him. In a hoarse voice, she said, "Come here, baby."

He had one second to think of whether he should do this slowly and sexily—perhaps in a way she'd always remember. Or he could do what his body commanded, what it burned to do. To jump on the bed, grab her, hold her, kiss her, bite her, and suck her.

And then a few other things.

A whole lot of other things.

Her left eyebrow quirked up. "Are you having second thoughts? I'm getting cold here."

He jumped onto the bed, and she came to him, meeting him. "I'll warm you," he whispered, putting his arms around her. "I'll build a fire inside you that will make you flame up."

She pulled her head back and laughed. "I'm hearing a lot of talk, but I'm not seeing a lot of—"

He pressed his lips against hers, stopping her words. At the same time, he pulled up the quilt so they could stretch out beneath it.

She was right; the women in his life were usually right.

It was time for action...

Twenty-one

Though most humans seem to enjoy sexual activities, their positions look awkward to me. ~Pooka

She couldn't stop the moans and groans coming out of her mouth, like she was a porn queen in a bad sex movie. He covered her with kisses and touches, until she couldn't stand any more, and she ordered him to *"Get inside me now!"*

He laughed, then put on a condom before following her order. In two strokes she was gripping his shoulders, and words that weren't words streamed out of her mouth. *"Ah ah ah ah ah."*

His body tense above her, he made a sound that was half laugh, half pain, as if all his attention was focused on one body part.

Good. She clutched his shoulders. *Good. So good, so damn good.*

And then he was moving faster inside of her. Touching all her hot spots. As if his penis was shaped just to do this to her. Because *oh, my goodness!*

Her hands clutched his shoulders tighter. No man had ever done this to her before, given her this many small orgasms, one after another, like little body-quakes.

She never wanted this to stop. She wanted to die like this.

He moved faster, the sensations multiplying. Her skin fully alive and aware. Every inch of her alive as he thrust into her, and she welcomed him.

Then she shattered. Her body pulsing. She wanted to scream, but her sex-fogged brain retained enough awareness of his daughter two floors up, and she made grunting noises instead.

"More!" she whispered, though she didn't know how he could do more. "More and faster."

He answered her, and she braced her feet and pushed her butt upward, off of the pullout bed, to meet his thrusts.

And then she shattered again, harder and higher, and so did he, his body heavy on hers as they both made whimpering noises.

She wrapped her arms around his back and her legs around his thighs.

They stayed like that as their bodies pulsed with aftershocks, each one slowing and muting. Their breaths and their heartbeats slowing, too.

Her legs slid off of him, and when he finally rolled off of her, she felt well used and too depleted to move. As if every muscle in her body had changed into mush. That included her brain, satiated and drunk from intoxicating sex.

He headed to the bathroom in the basement, staying in there a few minutes, and she guessed he was cleaning himself.

When he returned, she was still lying in the bed.

"There's a problem." He stood by the side of the pullout bed instead of flopping onto it.

She raised her eyebrows and tried to keep her gaze from moving downward. After all, it wouldn't be at its most glorious now, and she'd already seen everything he had. She hoped to see it again. Later. Though not *too* much later. But right now she had no energy for another round.

"That's not the words I like to hear after sex. But go on."

"It's not the words I'd like to say after sex, either." He paused, his eyebrows contracting. "The condom was torn."

She pushed up on her elbows, her heart beating fast again. She wanted to cry, but not with anger or sadness. It was the intense rush of *hope*.

Please, God, please give me a baby.

And not just any man's baby. If she was pregnant, it would be Adam's baby. *Adam's.*

"I had to tell you now," he said, "in case you want to go to the pharmacy and pick up the morning after pill."

Her breath sucked in. "Is that what *you* want?"

He didn't answer for a moment, and when he did, his voice was a harsh whisper. "I don't know if I can do this again."

"Do what? Be a dad?" She didn't want to say *husband*, because that would be too much to expect. If life had taught her anything, it was that she shouldn't expect too much. At the most, she'd learned to expect a peaceful, orderly life.

And look how well that had worked out, with a missing husband and a demolished house.

She patted the bed next to her, pushing back her unproductive thoughts that just made her feel sorry for herself. "Get in. You're cold."

He turned off the light by the couch before hunkering down next to her. Not touching her, but only inches away.

"It's tough to care so much," he said. "To watch their pains and their sorrows. And if they die..."

He stopped, and she knew he was thinking of Noelle's accident and Tori's diabetes.

The basement was dark, but she groped between them and found his hand, holding it.

"The odds that I'm pregnant are pretty low," she said. "For three years, Paul and I tried to get pregnant, and it didn't happen."

"I wasn't just talking about a baby," he said. "I was talking about you."

She closed her eyes tightly against the hurt that she felt, but the tears still leaked through.

When the tears stopped, she turned her back to him. "You should go to your bedroom."

"I didn't mean—"

"You'll want to be there when Tori wakes up in the morning."

There was silence, then the bed creaked as he rolled out of it and switched on the light. As he put on his clothes, she rolled to face the wall, her eyes open, her body tense.

"We'll talk in the morning," he said.

She didn't reply. She tried to empty her mind, because what was there to think of? The best sex ever, and then a gray mass of unhappiness.

Usually at times like this, she counted the best things in her life—which almost always started with Falco—but not now. Not so soon.

The boy she'd loved since she'd first seen him, who had turned into a man and a father, was a coward at heart.

She had been incredibly stupid.

"Do you want the lights off?" he asked.

"Yes. Let Falco come downstairs first."

He headed up the wooden steps, and, seconds later, Falco came down them, turning into the basement, his mouth open. Happy to see her. She reached out and held him, staying that way even when the lights went out. She was tempted to let him into her bed, but Falco had been trained to sleep on his big doggy bed on the floor. Paul's choice, but she had agreed with him. To reverse the training now would be confusing for Falco.

Finally, she whispered that he should go to sleep. She remembered Adam putting the carpet in with the help of his dad before he and Noelle had moved in. There was a thick pad beneath the carpet, and Falco should be comfortable. She kissed the top of his head and pulled away. He laid on the side of the bed nearest her, and she curled up on her side, staring into the darkness, unable to sleep, not wanting to think.

It felt like a long time had passed when she heard a car cruise up the narrow driveway at Josh's house next door. In the night's silence, she clearly heard the hum of the car's engine through the basement window. She focused on the sound. Better to think about that than her one-nighter and never-againer.

The hum didn't stop, though, and as the minutes ticked by, she began to be nervous. She assumed it was Josh's mother in the car, and if the car was running and the windows were closed, that could be a bad situation. His mother could be killed.

Of course she'd heard stories about Diane. Stories were cheap in Trouble Bay, and sometimes they were vicious. She imagined that after Paul had disappeared, the gossips had been busy talking about her marriage. And after the fire tonight, she knew that if anyone was going to be talked about, it would be her and not Diane.

It didn't stop her tension. If Diane remained in the car with the motor running and the windows most likely closed against the near-freezing air outside, she might be poisoned by carbon monoxide.

She rolled out of bed. Careful not to step on Falco, she stood. Falco got to his feet, too. Outside, a car door slammed, and a man's and woman's raucous laughter spilled through the basement window.

She winced. What an adult did and with whom she did it with were none of her business. But now that Lauren knew Josh and what a good kid he was, she cringed for him.

If Josh were her child...

But he wasn't, and it was likely she would never have one.

The laughter stopped, then a car door shut

again. The car engine revved up, and the car rolled out of the driveway.

She breathed easier. Nothing to worry about.

And then she remembered the broken condom.

Her heart beat faster. If she were pregnant, Adam wouldn't be happy. But to hell with him. She would be screaming and jumping with happiness.

She clenched her hands tightly. "To hell with him," she whispered. *"To hell, to hell, to hell."*

Her eyes had adjusted to the darkness, and enough moonlight shimmered in through the small windows to allow her to see. Trembling, she hurried to the chair where she'd dumped her clothes. She wasn't waiting for morning. She wasn't waiting for *anyone* anymore.

Clutching her clothes to her left side, she spread her right hand over her flat belly.

She'd had a long streak of bad luck. A cold marriage. No pregnancies. Her best friend killed. Her husband missing. Her house on fire.

The man she was crazy about had made love with her once...and then he was sorry.

Maybe it was time for her bad luck to be over.

It could start with a baby...

Twenty-two

Humans should know that the only one in charge of their happiness is themselves. ~Pooka

It was not a good day.

Even before he went down to the basement, Adam sensed that she was gone. And so was her dog. He'd felt the silence, the emptiness. She'd even switched the bed to a couch again, the sheet and quilt folded neatly on the sofa, and, next to them, two pillows, plumped up. His robe, T-shirt, and boxers on top.

He just stood there, though he knew he should leave the basement. He didn't want Tori to wake up and come downstairs and find him like this. As if he were frozen.

But he didn't move. All he could think of was what an ass he'd been last night.

What a coward.

Noelle, the most generous woman he'd known, wouldn't have wanted him to leave so rudely last night after having sex that was the best he'd had since... He couldn't remember. He couldn't compare Lauren with Noelle. It wasn't fair to Lauren. Nor was it fair to Noelle, his laughing wife.

Or the wife who'd sometimes cried and screamed at him.

He hadn't been perfect, either. Last night hadn't been the first time he'd screwed up.

But if Noelle hadn't died, they would have made it. He had no doubt about it. They'd been two imperfect people who loved each other and who loved their daughter.

He rubbed his hand down from his forehead, over his eyes, his nose, his lips, down to his chin. As if rubbing away the old memories. This wasn't about him and Noelle. This was about him and Lauren. Tall and slender Lauren, who looked like an aloof princess.

Not in bed, though. In bed, she'd been...amazing. Responsive. Passionate.

And he'd used a condom so old that it had torn.

She'd said it was unlikely she would be pregnant, but pregnancies happened. It was a possibility.

His heart thumped.

If she were...

He worried about one child.

And he worried about Lauren's house on fire.

And now she wasn't here, and he worried about what she might do.

Because he'd said the wrong thing last night, right after their sizzling lovemaking.

Just the thought of it made him hard, and if he weren't so worried...

Where was she? *Where the hell was she?*

He picked up the phone and punched in her number. It went to voice mail. "Lauren, are you okay?" he asked. "I have to know." He took a breath. "Are you okay? Call me. Let me know where you are."

He put the phone away before he said something even more pitiful.

What he'd already said made it sound like he cared.

He did. He cared too much.

It scared the hell out of him.

"Dad!" Footsteps clambered down the basement stairs.

He put on his dad face and turned to her. Her face was flushed, her eyes sparkling. She peered around the room, and the brightness in her face faded. He could feel the change, as if the air changed, too, from happy air to miserable air.

"Where's Lauren?" she demanded.

"I came down, and she's gone."

"Why did she leave? What did you do?"

"I didn't do anything."

"I know you were with her last night. I heard you walk down the basement steps."

He forced himself not to grit his teeth together and turn his gaze away from her. The same way he used to force himself to lie to his mother as a teenager. *"No, Mom, I wasn't drinking at the beach with the other kids. No, I didn't have to run away when the deputy came."*

"I didn't do anything," he said.

Tori glared at him, her brows knit together. Her angry face. Then she turned around to stomp up the steps. The precursor to her silent treatment.

He straightened his spine. Yes, it was going to be a bad day. He'd screwed up.

Now he needed to fix it. He needed to man up. He needed to... Oh, hell, he didn't know what he needed. A miracle, maybe. Sex apparently wasn't good for his brain, and he had screwed up big-time.

Twenty-three

If I were human, I would sleep all day and dance all night. ~Pooka

It was a bad day.

Wearing yesterday's clothes, all muted grays and blacks, including yesterday's underwear, Lauren sat in the Door County Sheriff's Office.

She didn't feel muted today. She felt angry red, upset purple, and shaky yellow. Not her usual sensible and neutral-colored self.

Damn it, she wanted her clothes.

She wanted her shower.

She wanted her morning coffee.

She wanted her *house.*

Just for today, she wanted to be like a child and sit on the floor, then kick her legs and flail her arms and scream as loud as she could.

Instead, she leaned to her left and put her hand on Falco's head. He was lying down, but his head and neck were up, making his head the perfect place for her to touch. Her canine connection to goodness and love.

For the hundredth time, she was grateful that she'd registered Falco as a therapy dog. She used the vest for the hospital because it was an instant visual verification to calm the most nervous parents. But Falco also had a tag hanging from his collar. This allowed her to take him inside the sheriff's office, and then this small room, where the only therapy was for herself.

Though that wasn't exactly true. Since they'd entered the building, almost everyone they'd passed had smiled at Falco. A few had reached out to pet him. Instant relaxation. Instant smile. Instant heart-warming.

"Great dog." Investigative Sergeant Cliff Nichols reached out to rub Falco's ear, affirming her theory. He was fortyish and balding, with skinny legs and a potbelly. Though she didn't know everyone in the county, they were acquainted. His wife was a nurse at the hospital, and she'd dragged him to a few fundraisers.

He pulled back and sat up, his expression changing from dog lover to stolid cop. She preferred the dog lover, but she sat straight across the table from him. Although there was one window—and on TV shows, interrogation rooms had no windows—she had the feeling that she was going to be grilled. An unpleasant experience she had reluctantly become familiar with after Paul's disappearance.

"Where were you when your house exploded?" Nichols asked.

"A friend's house."

"The name of your friend?"

She told him. His expression was blank.

Sturgeon Bay was the biggest city in Door County—the *only* city in the county—with a population just under ten thousand. Not exactly big, but too big for everyone to know everyone in the city, much less out of it.

"It's convenient that you weren't home," he said.

"Excuse me?" She sat straight. "It's *not* convenient to have my house blown up. All my clothes, my personal papers, my books, my paintings, my—" She sucked in her breath. Stopping. Putting her lips together to hold back the words. Maybe even to hold back the tears that were burning the backs of her eyes.

Nichols was staring at her. Waiting for her to add something, and she didn't know what. The truth? Okay, she'd tell him the truth. "I'm alive." She put her hand on Falco's head. "And so is Falco. I'm grateful for that."

Nichols raised his eyebrows. "When did you find out about the explosion?"

She put her hand back in her lap and told him.

"Why didn't you call us right away?"

"When I found out, I was too shaken to contact you."

"When you found out at your friend's house," he said. "Your *male* friend."

"Who I've known since I was a teenager." She stared at him, her chin up. "His wife was my best friend and—"

"*Was?*"

She took a deep breath. "She died in a car accident three years ago. I'm godmother to their daughter. I don't see them as often as I should, so the one time that..." Emotion overcame her, and she had to stop again, shaking her head, pulling in her composure.

Nichols waited, his own expression stoic, and Falco got to his feet, standing next to her.

Her hand slid down to his neck. Immediately, she felt more composed.

"Does the dog have to go out?" Nichols asked.

She turned to look at Falco, who looked back at her with his brown eyes. Love. That's what she saw in his eyes. And she loved him right back. "He sensed that I was upset. He's letting me know he's here for me."

"Does he bite?" Nichols asked.

"Not yet. I like to think that if someone threatened me, he would protect me."

"Any good dog should do that."

She slowly put her hands back in her lap and looked straight into his eyes. "That's what sheriff's people do, right?"

A grin flashed on his face, then was gone. "Are you comparing us to dogs?"

"No, but if I did, you should feel flattered. I have a very good opinion of dogs."

His grin grew. "More than people, huh?"

She reminded herself that although he was smiling and friendly now, she was being interviewed. No, not quite interviewed but *questioned*. There was definitely some suspicion in his questions. She could understand why. She had a missing husband...and now *this*. He had to be wondering why anyone would want to kill her.

That made two of them.

"I have nothing against people," she said. "I

work in fundraising, and for the most part, I find people generous and eager to help others."

His eyebrows climbed up. The sign of disbelief. She shrugged. Why not tell the truth?

"I'm sure there are bad dogs." She paused, and Nichols didn't interrupt. He was good. Very good. She leaned forward. "But I *know* there are bad people."

"Anyone you care to name?"

She shook her head.

"Your husband?"

"This isn't about Paul. He's missing, and I don't know where he is. I was questioned enough about it before."

"What other reason is there for anyone to want to blow up your house in an attempt to kill you?"

"I don't *know*." She heard the anguish in her voice, and she clamped her mouth shut. Not berating him. Not standing to leave. After all, she could go if she wanted. He couldn't hold her here. But she knew if she were in his shoes, she would wonder about her innocence, too.

He stared at her for a long moment, as if trying to see the truth in her face, the tension thick in the air. "You were telling me why you didn't call us."

"From what the newscaster said, the explosion had been set on purpose. And whoever did it must have thought I was inside the house." She swallowed before continuing. "About eight years ago, someone tried to break in while my husband and I were gone."

"So, this wasn't the first time?"

"It's the first time anyone tried to blow up my house."

"That's not what I—"

"Paul thought that it was a tourist. Or a kid hoping to steal something. A neighbor came out to put her beagle out, and she heard someone running away. When we came home, we found a broken window, but that was it. It didn't look like whoever it was had gotten inside." She frowned at him. "We filed a complaint."

"I saw the complaint. I wanted to hear about it in your own words. What else?"

"After that, we got in the habit of leaving the lights and TV on in the evenings when we weren't home."

"Besides your missing husband, have there been any changes in your life recently?"

She lifted her arm to scratch her neck, then saw his eyes shift, watching for signs of nervousness. And, perhaps, guilt. Once again, she lowered her hands to her lap, where he couldn't see her clutching her hands together.

"I'm starting the procedures to divorce my husband."

"Is there a reason for this now?"

"My husband and I had a prenup, and it ends in February."

"Ah. This is about money. What else would you like to share?"

"My parents always advised me not to talk about our finances."

"People only say that if you have too much money...or if you don't have enough." He leaned forward. "This information might be pertinent to our investigation."

"I'm not poor," she said.

"My grandmother, who lives in a cramped, one-bedroom apartment in a retirement home, thinks she's not poor." Nichols pulled his chair up closer to the table, still leaning toward her. Almost as if he were trying to get into her face. "I'm not asking how poor you are. I'm asking how rich you are."

"I'm not as rich as any of the Trumps."

"Mrs. Finney"—his tone was sharp—"once again, I'm not asking about how much money you *don't* have. I'm asking how much you *do* have."

She wanted to laugh but was afraid that once she started she might not stop. "You may ask, but I don't have to answer."

He scowled. "You just can't say it, can you?"

"I don't *need* to say it. It's really none of your business." None of his *damn* business, she wanted to say but didn't.

"You don't talk about it?" Nichols asked.

She shook her head. Not many people knew how wealthy she was, and she wanted to keep it that way. Not even Noelle had known when she was alive. And she certainly wouldn't mention it to Adam. Not that she didn't trust him. It was just that, well, she'd been happy he and Noelle and Tori liked her for who she was and not for how much money she had.

Her mother and father liked to say, *Money makes people look at you differently.*

Different was never good.

A memory flashed in her mind. Her mother crying, hanging up the phone, then turning to Lauren's father, who pulled her into his arms. Something he normally didn't do in front of Lauren.

"My own sisters," her mother had said. *"They*

148

only call me when they want something. Sometimes I wish we'd never done so well."

"They're showing their true selves. If the tables were turned, you wouldn't be asking them for money every time they wanted a new car. Sisters like that, you're better off without."

"Someone might know," Nichols said. "Your husband knew, right?"

She nodded. Because of the prenup, her money was her money and his money was his, like it or not. And he hadn't always liked it. An image lit up in her mind of Paul, his lips pressed into a thin line when he'd discovered how much she'd donated to the children's cancer wing.

It had been shortly before his disappearance. By that time, she hadn't cared much about his opinion.

"Is it possible he mentioned it to anyone?" Nichols asked.

Her stomach tightened. "It's possible. I really don't know."

"His ex?" he asked. "Wendy Finney. Were they still friendly?"

"They were amicable."

"Amicable? That's what my wife calls a feeble word."

"Your wife is a smart woman."

"Yeah. I'm a lucky man," Nichols said. "He has a son, too, right?"

"He does. Rodney's going to UW in Green Bay. Just last month, I sent him a large check to help with his tuition."

"If something happened to you, would your money go to him?"

"He's not the primary inheritor." She shivered, her muscles contracting, but she couldn't believe that Rodney would try to kill her. She *liked* Rodney. He'd taught himself to play the guitar, and he liked to make up lyrics that made his mother laugh. "You think the motive behind the explosion is money?"

"Money or something to do with your ex. There's still his disappearance."

Her throat closed. Her eyes burned with sudden tears, and she used all her self-control to hold them back. "I don't know," she said, and heard the thickness of tears in her voice, "why anyone would want to kill me."

He leaned forward. "You think your husband is alive and out there? Waiting for the ten years to pass?"

"I don't know, but I really don't think so. He'd be endangering his own business, which is worth something. And disappearing just isn't *like* him."

"Let's go back to his ex-wife."

She shook her head. As she did, Falco pressed his head against her arm. Giving her a silent message: *I'm here. I'll protect you.* She reached out to him again, raking her fingers through the shaggy fur on his neck. He leaned into her hand, wanting more.

She pressed deeper, the way he liked. A doggy massage.

Why weren't people more like dogs? The world would be a better place. Dogs didn't care about money. They cared about petting and walks or runs. They cared about affection. And they cared a lot about food.

"I don't see Wendy much," she said, "but when we talk, we're friendly. I can't see her killing anyone."

"*When* you talk?" he asked.

She nodded. Nichols had caught that quickly. He was smarter than he looked. And she was smart, too. Instead of answering him, she just looked at him.

"When was the last time you saw them?" he asked, his voice neutral, not showing any frustration he might feel.

She crossed her legs. This really was like a game of cat and mouse. And in this room, he was the cat, and she was the mouse.

"We normally just talk on the phone."

He sighed. "All right, when did you last *talk* to her."

"Last week, I think. She called to thank me for the check. I give her money from the agency for Rodney. But I do that every month. I also gave him money for tuition. This last summer, Wendy asked if Rodney could use Paul's boat, and I said he could have it."

"Anything else you gave them?"

Her hand stiffened on Falco's neck. "I gave him two rings of Paul's. I wanted to give him Paul's car, but Wendy was worried that if anything happened to the car, Rodney might be in big trouble. If Paul showed up, he'd be furious."

Nichols's eyes squinted. "That tells me a lot about your husband. What else?"

"I told him he could have Paul's snowmobile. Paul rarely used it, so Wendy agreed to that. I offered him Paul's clothes, but he didn't want any. Not even his leather jacket."

"In other words, you were giving him everything of Paul's."

She shrugged. She was feeling sick. Puking sick.

"Rodney wasn't greedy," she said. "He didn't ask for anything. It was my choice to send him money. Wendy's a bookkeeper. As far as I know, she makes a decent salary. She hasn't asked for anything for herself."

"Did Rodney turn away the offer of the snowmobile?"

"He's nineteen. What do you think?"

Nichols barked a laugh, then caught himself, his lips firming. "It sounds like he didn't want anything personal from his father."

She shook her head, remembering the stunned look on Rodney's face the weekend after his father went missing...

But a part of her brain niggled. Perhaps he was just a good actor. Perhaps it was a case of *like father, like son.*

How many clients had happily and falsely thought that Paul was giving them good service? It was only after about four years of marriage that she'd found out he would promise the moon...and give them moonbeams. He was counting on people not to read the terms and small print, and it was amazing how many people didn't.

Besides, who was she to complain? At one time, Paul had convinced her that he loved her, and that was as false as it could be.

She should have divorced him much sooner than this.

"Mrs. Finney," Nichols said. In a louder voice, he said, "*Mrs. Finney.*"

She blinked, feeling as if she weren't really here.

"Are you all right?" Nichols asked.

She nodded. Except for being sick to her heart, and knowing it was possible someone had tried to kill her, she was just peachy.

Well, at least it had led to great sex with Adam. The best she'd had. Always a silver lining.

Except for his reaction over the broken condom. Clearly he'd been sorry for what they'd done. That put some tarnish on the silver lining.

"If your husband did disappear to stop you from divorcing him," Nichols said, "who would he have told?"

She shook her head, and at the same time, she frowned.

"You're thinking of someone, aren't you?" the detective asked.

She shook her head again, but said, "I ran into his associate at the hospital. He seemed upset about my divorce plans."

"His associate? What does he do?"

She explained, and he frowned.

"More like a sales employee," he said.

"Not in this case. He's been running the office since Paul's disappearance. Taking care of Paul's clients. Of course, I compensate him."

"What's going to happen when your divorce is final?"

"A prenup works both ways. If Paul died, I would receive more of his assets, but since there's no body, all the assets will go to his son."

"That hardly seems fair. Who thought of those terms?"

"We both did. I don't need his money, and Rodney does."

The sergeant stared at her for a long moment, then leaned forward. "I'm going to be talking to the son and your husband's ex-wife."

"They'll corroborate what I've told you."

"What else should I know?"

"Nothing from me." She spoke emphatically.

"Where are you staying now?" he asked.

"A hotel."

"In Sturgeon Bay?"

She nodded and gave him the name of the hotel, then stood. "I think that's enough."

"What are you going to do now?" He stood, too.

"Get coffee. Go back to the hotel. Call my lawyer." She looked down at Falco, who was on his feet, standing next to her. "Walk the dog. Shop for new clothes. Go to work."

"Be very careful. It might not be a good idea for you to go anywhere alone."

She put her hand on Falco's head. "Falco will protect me."

"From a gun? Or an explosive device?"

She swallowed, feeling light-headed. Sick.

"And how will you protect him?" Nichols nodded at Falco.

She swayed, and Nichols was at her side. "Are you okay?"

"I'm fine." She raised her chin and stood straighter. "I'm just tired. I'll feel better after I have some coffee."

A few minutes later, she was in her car, Falco

in the back. Her phone vibrated, and she picked it up and looked at the name on it. *Adam.* She stared at it for a few seconds, then put it back in her purse and shoved it to the bottom.

It was still morning, and so far it had been a *very* bad day.

Twenty-four

Humans should stop overthinking and just be happy. ~Pooka

In the vegetable and fruit aisle of Food & More, Adam pulled out his phone and called Lauren for the third time this morning. The wind outside had a frigid bite, and he'd dropped Tori off at school instead of making her wait for the school bus on the corner. The DJ on the country music station had said there was a possibility of snow. Nothing surprising about that. Door County weather was like the first line of *A Tale of Two Cities*. It was the best of times in late spring, all summer, and early fall.

And then came the worst of times. Winter. Although the ice fishermen, hunters, skiers, and snowmobilers might argue with him about that.

He liked his ice fishing as much as any other swaddled-like-a-baby guy sitting over a hole in the ice, waiting for a fish to bite. Enjoying the silence and the sense that God was there in the icy air. But give him warm sun and a soft breeze any day. He didn't even mind the influx of tourists that increased the population of the county from approximately twenty-eight thousand to two hundred and fifty thousand. Without them, he wouldn't be able to do the work that helped him pay for Tori's medical expenses. He didn't care that his house was small. He cared that Tori was happy and alive.

The phone rang once, then twice as Sylvia Pascal, who owned the best bed-and-breakfast in the town, turned into the aisle, pushing one of the smaller carts. She was an elegant blond woman. In high school, some of the boys used to call her a MILF—a Mother I'd Like to Fuck. But not if her son, Chuck, was nearby. Chuck was about five years younger than Adam and his friends, but it wasn't cool to say that in front of anyone's son.

The phone was ringing a fourth time when the ring shut off and Lauren's automated voice told him to leave a message. He turned his back to Sylvia and lowered his head.

"Lauren, it's me. I'm sorry about last night. I was an asshole. I was wrong. I didn't mean what I said. Where are you staying? I'm worried about you. Tori is worried, too. Are you safe? Call and let us know."

He hung up, turned—and jumped back to avoid jamming his cart into Sylvia's.

Her eyebrows raised, she watched him coolly as he stepped back and mumbled an apology.

"Hello, Adam," she said. "I couldn't help but overhear your phone message."

He swallowed a groan. She must have ears like

a bat. He'd been speaking quietly into the cell phone. He felt for Chuck, who lived with her now that his roommate had a girlfriend who'd moved in, which meant Chuck had moved out.

In a town as small as Trouble Bay, news like that flew faster than a jet plane.

"Excuse me for mentioning it," Sylvia said, "but I have a reason. Were you talking to Lauren Maguire?"

"Lauren Finney."

"*Him*." Her voice showed her dislike. "Paul Finney. I keep forgetting she was married to him."

"Legally, they're still married."

"I understand he's missing and presumed dead." Her mouth pinched. "And now there's funny business going on that's not very funny. I heard about last night's explosion."

He nodded, wondering what she was getting at.

"I don't know where she's staying," Sylvia said, "but we have vacancies at our place right now."

He nodded again. Sylvia's bed-and-breakfast was the oldest and nicest establishment in Trouble Bay, and it did well—especially since she'd put in a new roof, new furniture, and whirlpool tubs. She was reputed to make the best breakfasts in town, too.

Still, it wasn't likely she did much business in November. If there were no tourists, there were no guests who needed to stay at her place.

"I know she has that Irish wolfhound," Sylvia continued. "She wouldn't want to put him in a pen. Unless she's with friends, it might be hard for her to find a pleasant place to stay. You should tell her that she could stay at my place and bring her dog. This time of year the rates are low. You'll be doing her a favor."

He held back a laugh. He'd always thought Sylvia was a savvy lady. Too bad Chuck had inherited her looks but not her brains. At least, that was the consensus. Adam suspected that Chuck was as smart as anyone, and he was just a happy-go-lucky guy who didn't have a lot of ambitions.

"It's a great idea," he said. If Lauren agreed, she would be closer to him. A thought entered his mind. "On the other hand, you might be better off calling her yourself."

An amused smirk made him wince. So she'd heard him apologizing for being a dick.

"Certainly. Would you give me her number?" She took out her phone. "I'll call right now."

As he mumbled off the numbers, Sylvia entered them on her phone, then angled away from him. Any other time, he would have moved away, but she had listened to him. Besides, she'd probably end up leaving a message for Lauren. On the off chance that she did speak to Lauren, he wanted to *know* what she said.

"Lauren, this is Sylvia Pascal from Trouble Bay. I heard about the explosion, and I wanted to let you know that I feel for you. I can only imagine how terrible you feel. I know that you must be looking for a place for you and your dog and—"

He was just turning away when she stopped. He snapped back around, looking at Sylvia's immaculate white-blond hair that barely moved as she nodded to whatever the person on the other end was saying.

"Certainly," she said. "Yes, it's unlikely anyone will be sneaking around. We are on Main Street, and we do have nosy neighbors. I'm sure they'll report to me if there are any strange cars. And if you're worried, we have firearms in the house. Chuck knows how to use them. You know my son, Chuck, right?"

She tilted her head slightly to the right, listening, then nodding again. "I'm expecting guests for Thanksgiving, but we have a suite left on the third floor. It comes with a whirlpool and your own kitchenette. I should warn you that I'll be visiting a friend in Madison over the Christmas holidays. Chuck will be in charge. He'll take good care of you."

Adam stiffened. Chuck was younger than Lauren, but only by a few years. Lauren was a beautiful woman, and Chuck wasn't ugly. As far as Adam knew, Chuck didn't have any enemies. In fact, he might even be more protective of Lauren than most. When Chuck was a kid, his dad had died young. Murdered.

Another murder.

No one had ever caught his father's killer. At the time of the murder, Adam was just a kid, but he remembered there had been several suspects. Supposedly Chuck's dad had liked to drink and gamble and have a good time. Some of his good times had been with other men's wives.

This had been a couple decades or so ago, but in a town as small as Trouble Bay, old scandals were not forgotten. Instead, they were chewed over, swallowed, and regurgitated.

Sylvia started talking quickly about her charges, nodding sharply, her tone crisp.

Adam waited, needing to find out if Lauren was staying at Sylvia's bed-and-breakfast.

He'd be lying to himself if he said he didn't want to have sex with Lauren again. But that wasn't the reason he wanted her nearby. He wanted to watch over her.

Someone had tried to kill her. It could happen again. And in a small town like Trouble Bay, the would-be killer was more likely to be spotted than in any other place.

Noelle would have wanted him to watch over Lauren.

And anything else that happened...?

Lauren had been Noelle's best friend. Would Noelle be happy to see them together? Or would she hate it?

Even as he thought it, he felt a warm rush. As if sunlight poured down on him.

Or love.

Whatever it was, he wanted to hold on to the feeling and not let it go. But even as he entertained the thought, the warmth washed away.

He exhaled a deep breath that he hadn't realized he'd been holding. The rush of love was like the pooka. Something else he didn't want to believe was real...

He didn't want to believe a lot in life. Tori's type one diabetes. Noelle's death.

And making love to Lauren last night...

That he wanted to believe in. He hadn't planned last night, but he wasn't sorry. It was a memory he wanted to keep. One that he would take out of the corner of his mind often and relive.

"Of course." Sylvia's clear voice caught his attention. "I understand. Yes. You have my number. Call us anytime."

She clicked off, dropping her phone in her purse. As she turned around, he straightened his shoulders that had drooped down.

"She said no?"

"She's thinking about it."

Twenty-five

Power can be dangerous. So can fear.
~Pooka

In her office, Lauren deleted Adam's three phone calls, not even listening to his messages, then deleted three more through the day.

She was tired of being hurt. She'd had enough. Enough for her whole life. Maybe she would find a group called All I Want Is To Love and Be Loved. She would join that group.

The workday was nearly over when she received another call with Adam's last name. But the first name wasn't Adam. It was Tori.

She grabbed the phone. She'd caught up her work and had been about to leave. Outside, the sunlight was fading, the sky turning gray. The dreariness suited her mood.

"Hi, honey." She forced a smile. Tori couldn't see her, but maybe the smile would show in her voice. "It was great seeing you yesterday."

"I'd hoped to see you this morning, too. Dad said you were gone when he woke up."

Over the phone, Tori's voice sounded like Noelle's when they'd been teens. The thought made Lauren's throat ache. "I had things to do. I had to find a place to stay. For now, at least. Then I talked to someone at the sheriff's about the explosion. You know. Normal stuff."

Tori groaned. "That's normal like my diabetes is normal. You should stay with us."

"Thank you for the offer, but I can't put you in danger."

"That's what Dad said you'd say."

Lauren stiffened. "Did your dad tell you to call me?"

"My dad's worried about you."

Sure he was. Worried about the broken condom.

There was an ache in her chest and then a moan to her side. She glanced over to see Falco getting to his feet, and she immediately felt calmer. She reached out her hand and put it on his head, and her whole body relaxed with the instant hand-to-heart connection.

She was able to bring Falco here because the aides or nurses often came to take him to see patients who needed cheering up. But she often suspected it was the nurse or the aide—and the occasional doctor—who needed cheering up.

It even worked for her, especially after someone had tried to kill her.

"I can't take the chance that whoever blew up my house"—she paused and looked into Falco's brown eyes, taking in the comfort—"would try to blow up yours, too."

"That's what Dad said you'd say."

Lauren pressed her lips together. That made two things Adam had warned Tori that she would say. He was definitely behind this call. She wanted to be angry, but at the same time, her lips wanted to stretch into a smile.

"If you won't stay here," Tori said, talking swiftly, "you could stay at Sylvia Pascal's bed-and-breakfast. You know, the big white house on Main Street?"

"I already talked to Sylvia." Lauren pictured the three-story bed-and-breakfast in her mind, and then the woman who owned it. She had always been a little in awe of Sylvia, who sometimes came to Lauren's fundraising events. Sylvia was attractive in a classical manner and always dressed beautifully, and when she spoke, it was usually about something that mattered.

"So you're coming?" Tori asked. "I know she said Falco can come."

Lauren's breath sucked in. "How do you know that?"

"That's what Dad said. Right, Dad?"

Lauren held back a groan. Adam must be *right there*. Right next to Tori. Maybe he was telling her what to say.

This was so...teenage-ish.

She should be mad. Instead, she smiled so widely her cheeks hurt.

"It's on Main Street." Tori said. "So it's going to be hard for anyone to sneak around there with a bomb without being seen. And Chuck is there now, so he can watch over you, too."

"I'm used to watching over myself."

"I know." Tori's voice was quiet. "I feel the same way about my diabetes. I hate diabetes, too."

Guilt spilled over Lauren.

"They have a whole suite," Tori said before she could apologize. "They have two suites on the top floor, but no one else is there now, so it would just be you until Thanksgiving. You and Falco. You would have your own sitting room. And a really pretty pedestal whirlpool bathtub with jets. Dad did some work there after lightning struck her house, and I got to see it."

"That sounds lovely, but I usually use the shower."

There was silence.

"I suppose I could try the whirlpool."

"Yay! That means you'll stay, right?"

Lauren laughed softly, feeling warmed and wanted, when just moments ago she'd felt cold and alone. Alone except for Falco.

"I'll go over there and check it out. I know Sylvia, and I've passed by the B-and-B often. The place I'm at now is fine, and they do allow pets, but..." But it was a hotel, and it felt like a hotel. Sylvia's place looked like a big, well-taken-care-of home. "I'll make a decision after I see it. Thank you for calling." She inhaled a deep breath. "And thank your dad for arranging this."

A squeal came from Tori. "I knew you'd come. And it's so close to our house. You can have dinner with us at night. Tonight would be good! Dad's making—"

"Tori, slow down. I'm still at work, and I have shopping to do. Everything I own that wasn't with me or at the office was destroyed."

166

"Oh, no. Books, too?"

"Yes, books, too. *Everything.*"

"That's so horrible. All your clothes, your shoes, your earrings. I didn't think of that."

Lauren nodded. It was all gone. Burned. Exploded. Demolished. She wouldn't miss her jewelry—she could buy new jewelry—and she was glad she'd uploaded her favorite old pictures to her digital photo storage.

Everything else was just...stuff.

"What I really need is underwear," she said.

Tori giggled. "What about dinner tomorrow? Can you come over?"

"Um, I'll probably be busy tomorrow, too."

"Are you sure you're not mad at my dad?" Tori asked, the laughter gone from her voice.

Lauren cringed. "I don't know who's doing this. I should stay away from you. I can't put you in danger."

"You know I have the pooka here, right? If anyone tries to blow up the house, Pooka would warn me."

"Honey..."

"And this is such a small town. It's hard to follow anyone around the town without being noticed. Someone would see him. Or her." A big sigh came from Tori's end of the phone. "Someone is *always* watching."

Lauren swallowed a laugh. She'd thought the same thing when she was Tori's age. Yet teenagers still managed to have parties that their parents didn't know about. Adults had their fun, too, and kept it from their kids.

Sylvia's late husband had been killed in

Trouble Bay after he'd left a bar late one night. His killer had never been found. Lauren had been young when it had happened, but she'd been old enough to know that he'd been a player and a drinker and a gambler. There had been plenty of suspects—and quite a few were angry husbands.

She wondered if Sylvia had felt the same sense of relief about her husband's death as Lauren felt about Paul's disappearance.

"We'll see," Lauren said. "I just don't want to get you in danger."

"Then you're not mad at my dad?"

"Why would I be mad at him?"

A huff of breath came from Tori. "I'm not dumb. When you ask those kind of questions, I know you're avoiding answering me."

"Tori! I—"

"Then come on Thanksgiving! It's the first time we're having it since Mom's been gone. My grandpa and grandma are coming—my dad's mom and dad. And then just us. Come, please. I want to see you."

"I don't know—"

"Falco can come, too. We'll have lots of scraps for him. I know I'll save a bunch for him."

"Are you trying to bribe me through my dog?"

"Is it working?"

Lauren laughed. "Maybe. Can I answer you later?"

"As long as the answer is yes! I've gotta go now. I'll tell Dad you're coming for Thanksgiving. And if I don't have a ton of homework, I can visit you and Falco at Sylvia's. 'Bye."

She hung up before Lauren could say

anything. Still holding the phone, Lauren turned to Falco. "Looks like we might be back in Trouble Bay again."

Falco made a sound in his throat, and she was sure he was talking to her. After all, he was exceptionally smart.

"I think you'll like Sylvia's place." A vibration shivered through her, as if she were a violin string that someone was plucking. "And I think so will I," she whispered.

If only someone hadn't tried to kill her, her life would feel so much better.

If onlys were always there, and she needed to hold her head high and persevere.

Her life was changing. But right now, with a missing husband and someone possibly trying to kill her, she was in a kind of limbo. She didn't know what to do to fix either of those problems. But one thing she knew for sure was that she didn't want to die. She wasn't ready. She hadn't done enough. She hadn't *loved* enough.

Her mind went back to the basement of Adam's house. Her and him together. The hot and wild and wonderful night.

And then his dismay.

Her agony and despair ran together, and she let go of Falco and wrapped her arms around her chest and rocked back and forth. Next to her, Falco whimpered, and she rocked one more time, then shuddered.

"We're going to be okay," she whispered to Falco.

He woofed. She bent down to kiss his head.

"If men were more like dogs," she said, "there would be a lot of happy women in this world."

She stood and picked up the phone to tell Ashleigh that she was leaving, and she would be taking off tomorrow, too. She had things to do. Clothes to buy.

Everyone had said she shouldn't have come in today. They'd been wrong. She'd needed the semblance of order at a time when her whole life was in disorder. If only to cancel appointments and reassign dates, she was taking a tiny bit of control of her uncontrollable life.

Damage control.

Maybe damage control was what life was about.

As she walked out, though, it came to her that this craziness had begun as soon as she'd started the preliminary process to divorce Paul.

Someone didn't want her to divorce him. Didn't want it enough to kill her.

Damage control, she reminded herself as she headed for the stairway, her teeth clamped together tightly and a dog at her side. She could get through this. She just had to be smarter than her would-be killer.

Smart enough to find out who it was.

Smart enough not to trust anyone.

And smart enough to stay alive.

Twenty-six

*If you don't feel good about yourself,
neither will anyone else. ~Pooka*

Tori sat on the end of her bed with her legs
crossed, wearing her turquoise fleece pants with
yellow ducks, because it was cold out and they
made her feel happy—and it wasn't as if anyone
was going to see her with the childish pants that
her dad *had* to buy her. He was clearly trying to
keep her a kid. It wasn't going to work, even if she
did like them.

"Can't you do something to help?" She gave
Pooka a stern look. "So far, all you've done here is
sleep."

Pooka opened one eye. "And what have you
done?"

"I called Lauren." Her voice rose. "I told her
about the bed-and-breakfast. If she goes there,
it's because of me."

"Then you should feel happy."

"But I don't know who put a bomb by her
home and exploded it," she said. "This makes me

so mad. I know you can do more. All you're doing is hogging my bed. Can't you find out who tried to kill her?"

"No." Pooka closed one eye and left the other open. "But I allow you sleep here at night."

"It's *my bed*." She wanted to scream, but if she did, Pooka would turn her head away and ignore her. And her dad would hear her and freak out. He'd come running up to see if she was screaming because she hurt herself or was dying or something.

She knew he worried about that because of her diabetes. He worried she might die like her mom.

But her mom hadn't had diabetes. It could happen to anyone. To her dad, even. He drove a truck most of the days. He was more likely to die than her. Sometimes when it was snowing or raining bad, she worried about him. Worried a lot.

The other kids in her class, they thought their parents would never die. She knew that they were wrong. Parents did die.

And then there was Lauren. Someone had already tried to kill her. What if they succeeded next time?

"You know what the problem with humans is?" Pooka asked.

"You told me yesterday. We're too greedy. But I'm not greedy, so you're wrong."

"You're young. Wait until you're a woman. See how greedy you are then."

Tori leaned over her knees. "I'll never be greedy. Never!"

"Then stop expecting the impossible. I can't

wave a magic wand and fix broken lives. I didn't make this mess. I can't clean it up and put it back together."

"I didn't make the mess, either."

Pooka raised her eyebrows. Not real eyebrows, but the furry ridge above her eyes looked like eyebrows.

"Maybe not, but your kind did. Humans think they're all-powerful. They think they're always right. They think they deserve everything. And if they don't get everything, you know what they do?"

Tori shook her head. She'd never seen Pooka like this before. "They kill people?"

"Yessss. Some do." Pooka hissed. "And some don't."

Indignation roiled inside Tori. She wasn't the one lying around, doing nothing. Not that she was going to tell Pooka that again. She was just a kid! How was she supposed to fix everything? "If you feel that way about us, why are you here?"

"I was sent here." Pooka laid her head on her paws, giving out a message that she was napping.

Tori smiled, because she knew Pooka was going to hate her next question. "So someone sent you?"

Pooka just opened one eye again. A malevolent eye. Like the eye of the wicked queen in a Disney movie. "You think I'd be here if I didn't have to be?"

"If you weren't here, where would you be?"

"Someplace warm would be nice." The eye closed. "With the sun shining down on me."

"And you'd sleep all day."

"Yessss."

Though Pooka said no more, satisfaction oozed out of her. As if just thinking about the sun made her happy.

"You're really here just because of me?" Tori asked, and to her own ears, her voice sounded small.

"Humans always think I'm here because of them."

"You're in my bed."

Both Pooka's eyes opened. "So I am."

"Why would you be in my bed if you weren't here for me?"

"Why did Goldilocks sleep in Baby Bear's bed?"

"Ha, ha, ha." Tori glared at her. How was it that a cat was smarter than her?

Pooka's whiskers twitched, and Tori was sure that Pooka knew her thoughts, but Pooka didn't say anything, so all she could do was sit here and fume.

Or she could sit here and *not* fume.

Was that what Pooka was here for? To show her that getting mad over things she couldn't change was just a stupid waste of emotions?

"If you really weren't here," she asked, turning the conversation back to Pooka, "would you really be in a warm place?"

"I would be somewhere else. I go where I'm sent."

"Where did you come from? And were you always a cat?"

Pooka's head rose. Kind of like a snake's head, only hers came with soft, midnight-black fur and her interested blue eyes didn't seem sinister. "No

174

human ever asked me before. A long time ago my ancestors were in Inisfail."

"*Inisfail?* I never heard of it."

"It's an island that's called Ireland now."

Tori knew her eyes were going wide. "Wow. That must've been a really long time ago. How old are you?"

The cat's eyes narrowed as she stared at her. Apparently she was touchy about her age.

"I think it would be cool to have seen so much," Tori said so fast that a couple words ran together, "and to be, you know, wise. Would you like to go back to Ireland? Did you love it?"

"It was all I knew then." The cat stared at her, unblinking. "It was years ago. Many, many years. Unlike humans, we don't count years. During this time, I have been a cat. Always." Her eyes flickered shut and then opened. "Once you're a cat, you don't want to change to anything else."

"Not even a bird? Birds can fly."

Pooka hissed. "I'm a cat. We *eat* birds."

"You've eaten *birds?*"

"I don't eat birds now." Pooka sighed. "I would, but I can't. I've changed. Humans have changed. A few have evolved. Many have not. We can only go forward, not backward."

"You know what I think?" Tori asked.

"You're going to tell me, aren't you?" Pooka sounded resigned.

"I think my mom sent you here."

Pooka's head stilled. Excitement shivered through Tori, but she held back from squealing and clapping her hands.

"It's true. She did, didn't she?"

175

"I can't tell you."

"You have to keep it a secret?"

"I don't know." Pooka's voice was petulant, the same tone that adults got when she asked too many questions.

"You think it's possible?"

"Many things are possible." Pooka laid down her head again and closed her eyes. "I'm going to sleep now. You can leave."

Though it was her room, not Pooka's, Tori pushed off the bed, hopping to her feet. Not because Pooka told her to go but because *she* wanted to leave.

She was only supposed to be up here to test her blood sugar and change, then go down and do her homework.

As she headed toward the door that she'd closed behind her, her steps in her slippered feet were quiet. If she stayed up here any longer, her dad would probably come up after her, checking to see if she was alive.

She reached the door and opened it—and there her dad stood, in the hall. His expression blank.

Twenty-seven

Why wouldn't anyone want to be a cat?
We're smart, we're beautiful, we can
climb, and we have claws. *~Pooka*

"You were talking to the pooka." Adam grimaced. Anyone hearing him would think he was crazy.

But the alternative was that his daughter was crazy.

Or that she was imagining things—which could be something to do with her diabetes, though he couldn't see how.

His preferred choice was that his beautiful and smart daughter—who normally was so matter-of-fact and so damn brave, no matter what life threw at her—was actually talking to a giant, invisible cat who liked to sleep on her bed and give her pithy advice that never seemed to actually tell her anything. Like pieces of the puzzle, with most of the pieces missing.

He reminded himself that Lauren's dog had seen, smelled, or felt *something*, too.

And it was possible he'd been bit or scratched by the pooka, though he didn't like to think about it.

"What did the pooka say?" he asked.

"You believe me."

"Of course. Didn't I tell you that already?"

"I wasn't sure if you really meant it." Her eyes shining, she reached up and hugged him, jumping away before he could hug her back. "I thought you might be humoring me."

"I'm not a humorous type of person."

She rolled her eyes. "If you mean funny, I know that, Dad."

"Hey!"

She giggled.

"So, are you ready to tell me what the pooka said?"

"Not much." She frowned. "She wouldn't even tell me if she was here because Mom asked her to be."

He was quiet for a moment. "I think it's true."

"You do?" Her face brightened. "You're not just saying that to make me feel good?"

"If it's possible, your mom would definitely send the big cat."

She beamed, and he was fiercely glad he didn't deny it.

"You know what else Mom might've done?" she asked.

He shook his head, suddenly cautious. Getting the sunken gut feeling that he might not like what she was going to say. Maybe he shouldn't let her think he believed in this... *stuff.*

"I think mom sent Lauren here, too."

Another punch-in-his-gut hollow feeling stopped him from talking.

"You okay, Dad?"

He nodded but looked around. As if expecting to see something.

Like Noelle's laughing face.

He shook his head, because that thought was crazy. His dead wife matchmaking for him? That was off-the-charts insane thinking.

Yet a small ache remained inside him. And he could hear a voice inside his mind saying, *It's what she would do. You know it.*

"Daddy? Are you okay, Daddy?"

He looked down at Tori's triangular face and the frown on her forehead. "I'm okay. It's just that... I can't believe your mom would do that."

"Then why did Lauren come over on the same day someone blew up her house?"

He opened his mouth to tell her that she'd come over because he'd asked her. Then he shut his mouth. That might prove Noelle's theory. At least, to her.

"See?" Tori powered the word out in victory. "In all this time since Mom's funeral, you never asked Lauren over. Not until the day after the pooka came to our house. And then nothing until the next week when you called her again. That day— the same day someone blew up her house—is the day you picked to ask her to dinner. And because you asked her, she wasn't blown up."

"You would make a great prosecutor," he said.

"I don't want to prosecute people. I want to save them." She paused, taking a breath. "Like you saved Lauren."

"Honey, I didn't—"

"Or Mom saved her." Her voice rose and thinned, tears not far away. "Or Pooka did. But I think *Mom* did."

Oh, shit. He didn't need this.

And neither did she.

"It's possible, honey." Even as he said it, he had to stop himself from wincing. This was all crazy. First the pooka thing, and now she believed that her dead mother was behind all of this.

"So, you think I'm right?"

"I think you *could* be right."

She frowned.

"What I was going to say," he said quickly to divert her attention, "was that Lauren wasn't the only one who was saved."

"Falco!" Her face lit up again, her eyes glowing.

"That's right." He breathed easier.

"Then it had to have been Mom. Remember how much she liked dogs? Especially Falco?"

He nodded, and he felt something change in the air. As if it were sparkling. He peered around but nothing was there.

"Dad? You're looking funny. You really mean it? You really believe?"

He forced the frown away from his forehead. "Honest?" Maybe he should be honest. It gave him a bad feeling to lie to her. "I believe that you see the pooka. And Falco saw something, too. But I can't, so it's hard for me to say for sure."

"Then you were lying." Her tone was flat.

"No. What I believe is that it could happen." He flipped his open hands toward her. "Look at all the people who believe in devils and angels and fairies."

"And walking on water." She giggled. "I'd like to walk on water."

He nodded. "And a whole lot of people fight wars because other people believe in different gods than they do. And no one says they're crazy."

"But that is crazy, Daddy."

"Except you," he said.

She giggled, and he exhaled with relief. It was going to be all right. He didn't know anything for sure, but he didn't have to lie about it.

"I wish Pooka talked to you, Dad," she said.

"Me, too." And that was no lie.

"And I wish Lauren would come to our house."

He just nodded, not able to say anything, because the need hit him hard. And it felt like it was more than lust. The ache inside of him wasn't just about sex. Though sex with Lauren had been...fireworks.

He hoped she said yes to Sylvia's bed-and-breakfast. At least then she'd be living nearby soon, if only for a while.

Twenty-eight

Change your attitude. Change your life.
~Pooka

Lauren moved into Sylvia's place the next day. She couldn't resist the combination of comfort and classic elegance, plus Sylvia's mix of welcome yet distance. And then there was Chuck's easy smile and friendship, but like his mother, he didn't step over her boundaries. People took note of his easygoing personality and assumed he was not the brightest bulb in the package. Lauren preferred not to assume anything.

The best part about it for her was that Falco fit right in. Though Sylvia wasn't super friendly with Falco, Chuck took him for runs in the morning before Lauren left for long days at work. She and Ashleigh were putting together a big Christmas fundraiser for the children's ward. That was only part of their end-of-the-year fundraising, but it was Lauren's special project. In her first year at the hospital, she had had the idea that pcoplc's hearts opened up at Christmas, especially for children. And when their hearts opened, so did their wallets.

For other people, Christmas was for families. For her, it was for fundraising. And if some people did it for a tax write-off near the end of the year, that was okay with Lauren, too.

She really was busier than normal, and for her first two weeks at Sylvia's, she used this to avoid calls from Adam and Tori. But now it was Thanksgiving, and she had the whole week off. All of her invites for the fundraising were out, and unlike the doctors, nurses, aides, and so many people who worked in the hospital, her job wasn't necessary for the day-to-day operation. She wasn't needed.

How ironic that she was paid better than most of the men and women who did the real life saving and life-caring. It certainly showed what the hospitals valued most. Though she wasn't complaining, she did see the injustice.

Now she was on her way to one of the last places she wanted to be. Adam's house. Only because she couldn't think of a good reason to tell Tori why she wasn't coming.

Because your father doesn't love me, sounded whiny and inappropriate. Even more inappropriate would be, *And I made a big mistake of having hot and crazy sex with him. I really want to do it again, but I won't, because I know I'll get hurt.*

This wasn't the first time her good manners had gotten her into an uncomfortable spot. She needed to learn to be gruff like a mountain goat about Adam instead of a puppy who jumped up and down with glee, giving the silent message: *You like me! You like me! I like you, too. In fact, I think I love you.*

She pulled up at the curb. There was a hatchback in the driveway, and she thought it belonged to Adam's parents. Noelle's parents were living in California now, near Noelle's older brother and his family, so they wouldn't be here. As she got out of her car, the frigid wind cut into her face like icy knives. Her head down, she and Falco barreled up the walkway to the front door.

Tori opened the door, her eyes bright. "You came!"

"I said I would." Lauren stepped inside, Falco right behind her, a bottle of wine in her hand. It was frigid outside, the wind icy, and she was grateful for the instant warmth.

"Dad thought you might chicken out. Are you mad at him?" A horizontal line wrinkled Tori's forehead. "Dad won't say that you are, and you won't say, either. I wish one of you would tell me."

Lauren couldn't say anything, frozen by conflicting emotions that made her feel at war with herself.

"Happy Thanksgiving." Josh strode down the hallway from the kitchen, holding out his hand and bending slightly for Falco to sniff. At the same time, he looked up at her. "I can hang up your coat."

Tori's cheeks reddened. "I can hang up her coat."

"I said it first. Besides, I'm a boy."

"And girls can't hang up coats?" Tori narrowed her eyes at him.

"Sure, you can. But that's stuff a boy does."

Lauren snapped to life and shrugged out of her jacket, handing it to Josh. "Don't argue about who hangs up coats," she said to Tori. "When it's about pay inequality, or rights inequality, that's when you should argue loud and clear."

"I agree," said a rustier, feminine voice. Sandy, Adam's mother, strode in from the kitchen, wearing jeans and a green sweater. She looked good, with only a few lines on her forehead and the outer corners of her eyes. Her hair was blond now, though the last time Lauren had seen her at Noelle's funeral, her hair had been dark red.

They hugged tightly, and Sandy looked at her with moist eyes. In Lauren's ear, she whispered, "So glad to see that Adam is moving on with his life."

Lauren stared at her, but with Tori watching her so closely, she couldn't say anything. "Um..." She held out a bottle. "I brought wine."

Then she and Falco were herded toward the kitchen by Sandy and Tori, with Josh following, as Sandy said, "Adam and Hogan insisted on roasting the turkey, but I made the sweet potato casserole and the stuffing."

"I made the pumpkin pie last night," Tori said.

"I made apple pie," Josh said. "It's my grandma's recipe."

"Where's your mom, honey?" Sandy asked, something that Lauren had wondered but felt uncomfortable asking. "She's not working today, is she?"

His face flushed. "She's with a friend."

There was a pause, and Lauren patted his

shoulder. "Looks like we're both in the same predicament. I'm glad you're here, too."

He looked down, shoving his hands in his jean pockets, not saying anything.

Tori dropped back to his side and gripped his forearm. "I invited him. That's why he's here."

Uh oh, Lauren thought. *Uh, oh.*

Then she looked forward, and Adam stood in front of the open dining area with the long table behind him set with dishes and silverware and glasses. But he wasn't looking at Tori and Josh. He was looking straight into her eyes.

She felt her heart drop to her stomach.

Uh oh, she thought. *Uh oh.*

Twenty-nine

I see Earth as a giant napping spot.
~Pooka

Adam hadn't known what to expect during the dinner, but it went well. Just not smoothly. Smooth was no longer an expectation. At one time, smooth had been a given; now it was an abnormality. But so far tonight, his mom and dad had been great. His mom especially couldn't hide her glee that he'd invited Lauren.

A woman not related to him.

A woman her granddaughter already loved.

A woman who was smart and kind and not slutty.

So what if someone had tried to kill Lauren?

So what if she was still legally married?

His mother had her priorities, and she wanted to see her son and granddaughter happy again. So the hell with the small stuff. And when they sat down to eat, she'd steered Lauren to the empty chair next to his and said, "You sit here."

As for his dad, though his eyes twinkled when

he looked at Lauren, he had turkey, stuffing, and pie to eat, and beer to drink. Those were his priorities. To top it off, the Packers were going to play tonight, so he was a happy guy. The only thing that could ruin his mood would be if the Packers lost. And the only thing that would make the day better would be if he could teleport to Lambeau Field to watch the game himself. Without paying for the tickets, of course.

This was Adam's third Thanksgiving without Noelle, and the first since then that he didn't feel like he had fallen into a deep, dark pit that he couldn't climb out of. The first Thanksgiving he didn't feel a need to pretend for Tori's sake that he was feeling halfway normal and halfway happy. The first in which he gave heartfelt thanks, and he meant every one.

He still wasn't sure what normal looked like, and he still knew it wouldn't look like him. But since Lauren's last visit in his house, he'd crawled out of that dark pit and into the light. Too much light at first for him to believe it was real. But now he was ready to look at the light. Ready to embrace it. Ready to embrace Lauren.

All through dinner, he kept stealing glances at her. Small, quick glances so no one would notice.

And every time he did, his heart thumped, and his skin warmed from the inside out.

He'd been an idiot. He knew it. He'd driven her away, and he was lucky she'd come back to his house.

He owed that to his daughter, who was talking to Josh now while Josh was shoving turkey into his mouth.

For a second, Adam forgot about his own feelings as concern about Josh made him frown. Not much he could do for Josh except to be there for him. Josh had turned out to be a great kid, and it was too bad his mom wasn't there for him. No one knew who his dad was, so he couldn't get help there. And this was in a town where everyone thought they knew everything about everyone else's life.

Adam's mom announced it was dessert time. Lauren got up to help his mom with the pies. As they stepped away from the table, he remembered a Thanksgiving about twelve years ago when he'd overheard Lauren and Noelle in the kitchen after the meal.

"You know what I hate?" Lauren asked.

"I know I hate brussels sprouts. I just don't like the way they taste. What do you hate?"

"I hate that women do all the drudge work while men stuff their faces and then watch football and drink beer and eat more food."

Listening to them from the hallway, he'd cringed. The reason he was standing in the hall was because he was about to go in and grab beers for Noelle's dad, his dad, and himself. He was guilty as hell.

He stood straight, about to step inside and offer to help instead. But then Noelle spoke.

"You know what I like about Thanksgiving?"

"What?"

"I like talking with you while we do dishes. Otherwise I'll have to watch TV, and you know I really hate football."

They giggled, and in the hallway, he'd smiled.

A piece of pumpkin pie with whip cream on top was plonked down in front of him, and he blinked, back to the present. Once again, there was no soul-breaking sadness. Once again, he didn't have to fight back the darkness.

Instead, he smiled. It wasn't because he loved Noelle less. It was because the memory of her was like a balm inside of him instead of a knife in his heart. If Noelle were watching him, that would please her. She wouldn't want her memory to hurt him. She would want her memory to make him happy.

"Adam, aren't you eating pie?" his mom asked. "You love pumpkin pie."

"He's not a kid anymore." His dad's voice was gruff. "He can eat dessert later."

"You know how Adam is about desserts. If he's not eating one, there's something wrong."

"I'm eating." He scooped up a piece before she started talking about all the candy he used to collect on Halloween when he was a kid. A story everyone here had heard from her about five hundred times already. "I was just thinking of something."

"Something good?" his mom asked.

He looked at her for a long second, and in her face, he saw the worry and the hope mixed together. He nodded. "Yeah, something very good."

There was a silence. A hush. He glanced around, and the others were staring at him, hope on their faces. The same hope on his daughter's face next to him.

Except for Josh, whose eyebrows contracted in puzzlement.

And Lauren, who was staring down at her cherry pie as she precisely cut out a piece with the side of her fork, with all the attention of an explosives expert defusing a bomb.

He reached over and took her hand and squeezed it. She looked up, and for a few seconds, they stared at each other.

Then, suddenly ravenous, he released her hand and started in on his pie.

Thirty

Why pick just one day to be thankful?
~Pooka

"You're right," Tori said. "I'll be thankful
every day."

The pooka sighed, knowing it would
never happen. After all, Tori was only
human. ~Pooka

On the TV screen, the pregame excitement was over, the game about to start when Adam left the living room and headed into the kitchen to make his winning move.

"What are you doing here?" his mother asked, standing in front of the sink with Lauren next to her.

Lauren raised her eyebrows at him, as if he was the last person she expected to see in the kitchen.

"I'm here to help with the dishes," he said.

His mom dramatically crossed her hands over her breastbone. "Did I die and go to heaven?"

Lauren sputtered a laugh, but the look she shot him was wary.

Adam swiped his mother's towel out of her hand. "You deserve a break. I know you love football. Go watch it with Dad and the others."

"What about Lauren? Doesn't she deserve a break, too?" His mom winked at him.

"Ask Lauren if she'd rather wash dishes than watch football." Looking at her, he saw the struggle on her face before she shrugged.

"I hope the Packers win," she said to Sandy, "but I'm not really a football fan."

His mother beamed at her, then at him. He could practically see his mother's imaginary picture of him and Lauren in her mind, holding hands and chastely kissing.

An image of Lauren and him was already in his mind, and there was nothing chaste about it.

"If you want to watch the game, I'll dry." He turned to Lauren. "You join the others, too. Even your dog's in the living room watching TV."

"That's because they're eating," Lauren said. "I'll bet you money that someone is sneaking him food."

"Your dad." His mom made a huffing noise. "He eats like a pig. Falco's probably sitting at his side, waiting for crumbs."

"Good. Then I won't have to vacuum." As Adam talked, he kept his eyes on Lauren. "Are you going, or are you staying?"

She turned to the sink, reaching for one of the china plates from his grandmother's set that his mother had gladly passed on to him so she wouldn't have to hand-wash dishes during holidays.

Noelle had been thrilled. She used to love taking out the dishes for special holidays. If he'd sold them or given them away, he would've felt as if he'd betrayed her. Oddly, more of a betrayal than making love to Lauren.

"I'll stay." Lauren grabbed a dish. "You know me too well."

His mother nudged him, giving him a wink before heading to the living room.

"I don't know everything about you," he said to Lauren, ignoring his mother's wink. He was an adult now, but he wasn't so sure about his mom.

"What don't you know?" Lauren set the plate in the dryer rack.

"If you've had your period yet."

Reaching for a plate, she froze. "Yes," she whispered. "Yes, I did."

He heard sadness in her voice. Of course, he'd known about Lauren's struggles to get pregnant, even before she'd mentioned it to him in his basement. Having met Paul, he had his own opinions about that. For a second, he was sorry the broken condom hadn't turned into a baby.

He pulled her to him and held her close.

She was stiff against him, stiff beneath his hands...and then she melted, her face pressed against the shoulder of his corduroy shirt.

"It's okay." He patted her back. "It's okay."

"I don't know why I'm acting like this." She drew away from him, stepping back. Her eyes didn't have any tears, but he saw the redness.

"Because you want children," he said.

She groaned. "Noelle told you, right?"

"She knew I could keep my mouth shut. That hasn't changed."

She turned back to the sink. "My tests came out all right, but I'm older now. My chances to get pregnant will be even lower."

"You can adopt."

"Paul didn't want to adopt."

"Paul was an asshole."

As she snorted a laugh, he reminded himself that Paul might be alive, though he couldn't understand how a man could be alive and desert his son and his wife.

"He *has* a son," he said, purposely using the present sense this time.

"I know. Rodney's a great kid."

"Was Paul close to him?"

She shook her head.

"Have you considered that Paul might have had a vasectomy?"

"He said he didn't. But, yes. At the end, before he disappeared, I did suspect that might be the case."

"I wouldn't do that."

Her breath sucked in. She stared into his eyes. "Are you saying..."

"No. Maybe." He glanced down, and her hands were at her sides, curled tightly, the washcloth clutched in her right hand. He looked up again, straight into her eyes. "I have to be honest with you. I don't know."

Her eyes glimmered with tears. She raised her hand and tossed the washcloth into the sink. "I can't do this. You wanted to do the dishes. Good."

She snapped around, her hair swirling around her neck, and stomped out of the kitchen.

He watched her. Knowing that, once again, he'd screwed up.

Was he in? Or was he out?

He wanted in. He wanted in so much that it hurt.

And he also didn't want in. Didn't want another baby. Didn't want his heart broken again.

Thirty-one

For many humans, the more they have,
the more they want. It's not their lives
that are empty; it's their souls. ~Pooka

The front entrance of the bed-and-breakfast was unlocked. Lauren could hear the four couples, all friends, their voices boisterous. Pretty sure she was the last one in, she locked the door behind her, then stepped into the living room. The temperature outside was close to freezing, and she was glad for the warmth inside.

The couples called her and Falco over, offering wine to her. One man at the end of the couch kissed the top of Falco's head, saying he missed his dog. His face scrunched in a pre-cry mode as his wife called out an invite to Lauren and Falco to sit with them.

She thanked them and declined, hurrying away before the woman's husband started sobbing. She didn't judge him. She loved her dog more than people, too. Most people, anyway.

Especially more than men. Especially after tonight.

But a glass of wine sounded like a good idea. Instead of going upstairs, she headed into the kitchen to get a glass from the fridge, Falco following her. She would leave Sylvia an IOU.

The light was on, and she halted to see Sylvia seated at the table in the corner, an open book on the tabletop in front of her. She still looked lovely, but there were circles under her eyes. The kitchen smelled like the pumpkin pie that Sylvia had made to take to the posh resort where she'd had dinner with friends who were somehow related to her. In the small town of Trouble Bay, there were quite a few relations like that.

Unlike many of the locals, Lauren's family wasn't from the area. Her parents were both only children from small families. When she was fourteen, they had moved here from Kenosha, Wisconsin, for the beauty of the county and the low crime rate. Her parents hadn't needed to work, but they were musicians—her mother played flute and her father played trumpet—and they had been music educators at a local high school. When they were offered positions in Door County's Wine Country Orchestra, which only played about six times a year, they had happily agreed.

They'd stayed ten years before moving to Florida. When Lauren had told them she wanted to remain in Door County, they hadn't tried to convince her to go with them.

Normally, she didn't miss having a close family. But this had been a tough year.

"We're both back early," Sylvia said.

Lauren smiled, though she suspected it looked more like a grimace. "Do you mind if I pour myself a glass of wine? You can add it to my bill."

Sylvia's eyebrows rose. "It was that kind of a dinner?"

Some things hurt too much to talk about, and Lauren headed to the fridge, opened it, and took out a bottle of cranberry wine.

"I'll join you." Sylvia stood. "The wine is on me. Today I was making changes in my future."

Without a word, Lauren plunked down the bottle on the table, took off her coat, draped it over the chair, then sat across the table from Sylvia. She'd much rather listen to Sylvia's story than think about her own life.

Falco laid down next to her, a sigh coming from his mouth, as if he'd had a long day.

There was silence while Lauren unscrewed the top of the wine bottle, and Sylvia got the wine glasses and poured for both of them.

Lauren took a sip of her wine. It was sweet and light, just right for her. She wasn't much of a drinker, but tonight she felt like gulping down the entire bottle. With a sigh, she set down the glass and turned to Sylvia. "Want to talk about it?"

"I've got a fellow," Sylvia said.

Lauren leaned forward, perking up.

"He's a professor at UW in Madison. He's been coming up a lot, but this was a bad time for him to leave, and we had guests here. I missed him." The corners of her lips lifted. "And he missed me."

"You're going to see him?"

Her lips curved higher. "I'm going to live with him for the winter. I'm leaving on Sunday."

Lauren picked up the glass and swallowed. Sylvia's confidence that nothing would happen had kept her feeling safe. Which was ridiculous, because Sylvia couldn't know for sure.

"Should I find another place to stay?" Lauren asked.

"Not at all. Chuck will be here."

Lauren stared at her. Chuck, with his big smile, his toned body, blond hair, and a face like a sun god, had the looks to be a hero. Or even a superhero, if he wore the right superhero suit. But nothing else about him shouted that he was an avenger. Though she thought there might be a lot of substance in him, he wasn't showing it yet. Instead, everything about him said he was a good-time guy. And she wasn't looking for a good time.

"I know what you're thinking." Sylvia gave her a stern look. "You're wrong. If push comes to shove, Chuck will be there for you. In fact, this will be good for him."

Lauren nodded, though what she really wanted to do was gulp. Or scream.

"Chuck and I talked about it already. I have cameras in the front, the back, and the sides of the house."

"Because of me?" Lauren asked.

"I had them installed a year ago. I'm not a trusting woman. I'm a careful woman, and I combine carefulness with suspicion."

"I like that combination."

Sylvia's shoulders relaxed. "So does my guy."

"Are you two serious?"

"Serious as any woman in love. He's lighthearted. He makes me laugh." Her lips curved, and her eyes stared at the wall. Lauren grimaced. She knew Sylvia was picturing her man friend.

Sylvia shifted slightly, and the dreaminess on her face cleared. "You are staying here when I'm gone, aren't you? This shouldn't make any difference."

Lauren lifted her wineglass. "My house was blown up after my lawyer sent someone out to ask about Paul's whereabouts. A precursor to filing for divorce. Now I need to post three notices of my intention to divorce Paul. One post a week." She took a big gulp of wine. When she put it down, she heard a raucous burst of laughter from the living room, and Sylvia was staring at her. "I don't think I should take a chance that someone might blow up your beautiful place."

"My son," Sylvia said, strength vibrating in her voice, "will not let you down."

"I'm not worried about him letting me down. I'm worried about him being killed because of me."

"You underestimate him. A lot of people do."

Lauren sat back, wondering how many glasses of wine Sylvia had drunk.

"He's an expert marksman," Sylvia continued. "I taught him myself."

"With a handgun or shotgun or rifle?" Another option hit Lauren. "Machine gun?"

Sylvia snorted with laughter, something Lauren had never seen her do. "Not a machine gun. A pistol, though he does go duck and deer hunting."

Lauren nodded. Quite a few men in Trouble Bay—and quite a few women—knew how to shoot and hunt.

"You'll be protected." Sylvia leaned forward. "You'll stay."

"Um..."

"That was *not* a question." Sylvia narrowed her eyes. "And you know what else?"

Lauren shook her head.

"He'll teach *you* how to shoot a gun, too."

"Me? I don't—"

"You want to stay alive, don't you?"

Lauren nodded vigorously.

"Then you'll learn how." Sylvia yawned, putting her hand over her open mouth, then pushed up to her feet. "It's settled then. You're staying."

Lauren nodded again. "I'm staying."

Sylvia pointed her finger at her. "And you'll take shooting lessons."

Lauren nodded.

"Nothing else. I can already see that you're not for Chuck." Her head tilted to the side, her lips curved downward. "If you tried, you'd break each other's hearts."

"In that case, I won't try."

"Good idea. I'm going to bed. Alone tonight, but not much longer. Night." She turned and tottered toward the back hallway that led to her bedroom.

Lauren watched her until she turned into the bathroom. Not quite drunk but getting there. The bathroom door closed, and Lauren put the screw top cap back on the bottle.

Thanksgiving was over.

Good. With her house burned down, she didn't feel very thankful this year.

And then there was Adam, playing hot and cold.

She didn't want to play the hot-and-cold game.

She picked up her glass of wine to take it to her bedroom, and Falco, who'd been lying on the wooden floor, got to his feet. Her giant, loving dog.

"I'm lucky," she whispered. "I've got you."

They headed to the front of the house and up the stairs as she reminded herself that though she may have been unlucky in human love, she was very lucky in dog love.

And apparently, if Sylvia remembered this tomorrow, she was going to learn how to shoot a gun.

Her teacher would be one of the best-looking men in Wisconsin.

That made her luckier yet. She just had to make herself believe it.

Thirty-two

The problem with most humans is that they've forgotten how incredible they are. ~Pooka

Sunday. Church day. As usual, Adam went to Sunday services with Tori. It was good for her to be in a community of people who knew her and cared for her.

For himself, he took no joy in it, but today it had nothing to do with God allowing his wife and his daughter's mother to be taken away. He'd stopped railing at the big guy in the sky about the beginning of last year, and most of the bitterness was watered down.

He'd just gotten tired of being angry at God.

No, the only one he felt angry at today was himself.

He'd screwed up with Lauren. He knew that. He wanted her. She wanted him. And it wasn't that he felt unfaithful to Noelle, because he knew that Noelle would be delighted if he hooked up with her best friend and their daughter's godmother.

Besides, he couldn't forget that someone had blown up Lauren's house. Pete Masters, the local deputy who'd been assigned to Trouble Bay after a murder the last Fourth of July that still hadn't been solved, had told him the explosion was most likely a one-time thing. Pete had talked to the sheriff's people in charge of the case, and they had nothing to go on. In case they were wrong, Pete said he was keeping an eye on Lauren. Which, in Adam's opinion, meant that Pete cruised by Sylvia's B-and-B every day.

Though Pete was a good guy, he did not impress Adam. Since Sylvia's bed-and-breakfast was on Main Street, Pete would've had to drive by her place anyway.

After the services were over, Adam and Tori stayed to chat and munch on food that the congregation had prepared. A woman about a decade younger than Adam flirted with him. That was uncomfortable. Though she was attractive, he remembered her when he was a teen and his first girlfriend babysat for her. As usual when this happened, he smiled stiffly and kept shooting desperate glances at Tori, sending silent messages that he needed rescuing.

Normally she picked up on them quickly, but she showed her anger by turning her back to him. Finally, he said his daughter needed to leave, and he hurried off before the woman could invite him to listen to the "fab bar band" she kept raving about. Right now, the only music he wanted to listen to was the country station in his car.

"Thanks a lot." He hustled Tori outside to the parking lot.

"I'm not your defensive guard," she said, a smirk in her voice.

"Wait until the boys come after you."

Her cheeks reddened, and he was sure it wasn't because of the cold wind. "If Lauren had been with us," she said, "then the women would leave you alone."

"Well, she wasn't."

They reached their car and scrambled into it. Seconds later, their seat belts on, they headed out of the parking lot and onto the street.

"Pooka said," Tori began, then stopped. "Dad, don't roll your eyes."

"I wasn't rolling my eyes, I was checking to see how much gas we had."

"Then why were your eyes rolled up?"

"What did the cat say?" he asked, five words that up to a couple months ago he would never have expected to come out of his mouth.

"Do you *really* want to know?"

"I asked you, didn't I?"

"Okay. Then you should listen to me."

"I'm listening." *Get it over with.* He could feel her gaze on him, and tried not to think of anything, because she seemed to be reading his mind this morning. She was almost thirteen. A teenager. God help him, why couldn't she stay twelve for a few more years?

"Pooka said something really smart, Daddy."

"What's that? I really do want to know."

"*Really?* Okay then. She told me that your heart had been frozen."

He gripped the steering wheel, his breath gone.

"And now it's in the process of unfreezing."

He slowed the car for the stop sign by Main Street, then stared at her. She stared back until a car beeped behind him. He checked the street for traffic, then turned toward home. Neither of them said anything, but as they passed Sylvia's place, he slowed the car. Lauren's car wasn't on the street. He knew she didn't go to church, so it was probably in the back.

Not that it mattered. He couldn't do anything right now except to head home mindlessly, as if the car was driving on its own power. Which was just as well, because how could he think with his half-frozen heart pounding so hard and so fast?

He kept on going, because that's what he always did. Moving forward. Not thinking, because thinking often led to feeling. And feeling led to desperation.

The car pulled into their driveway. Finally.

"What did the pooka say I should do?" he asked.

"She didn't say. I could ask her, but don't you think you should figure it out yourself?" Tori unfastened her seat belt. "You know, Dad, it's weird that you're asking a pooka to fix your life."

She opened the door and jumped out of the car, but he remained in it.

So this was his life now. The weird guy who believed in pookas and had a half-frozen heart.

The guy who was screwed and needed to wake up and do something.

Because if he didn't, his half-melted heart might freeze up all over again.

Thirty-three

Every pooka knows that, for the most part, humans are pitiful creatures. If only they knew it was a choice, they might choose glorious. ~Pooka

Sunday morning, Lauren woke early and joined Sylvia and Chuck in the kitchen. It wasn't a place for the normal guests, but on Lauren's first night there, Sylvia had said that Lauren wasn't normal, which had made Chuck laugh, and even Lauren had smiled.

No, she wasn't normal. She knew Sylvia and Chuck, and she wasn't a seasonal visitor. She was homeless and almost pathetic, but they didn't make her feel pathetic. They made her feel welcome. A friend, albeit a paying friend.

Lauren fed Falco, then drank her coffee as Sylvia watched Chuck prepare the breakfast, nodding when he did everything right. Sylvia put on her coat, hugged and kissed Chuck, then hugged Lauren, too.

She didn't hug Falco, but she respectfully said

good-bye and gave him a scratch behind his ear.

And then she was gone. On her way to her lover in Madison. Lauren couldn't help thinking that this was not the Sylvia her parents had known. She'd always admired Sylvia, but now she admired her more, and she wished her well.

The guests came down an hour later. Everything was ready except for the scrambled eggs, which Chuck made in a short amount of time. Checkout was eleven, but it was nearly noon before the guests left. Smiling amiably, Chuck didn't mention the delay as he helped the guests with their suitcases, though he didn't need to help. In the driveway, he lightly flirted with the women, who were about fifteen years older than him. All done with good humor, and he was as attentive to the two heavier women as he was to the curvy one and the model-slim one.

Lauren was impressed. The husbands were grinning, not upset. Maybe because with them, Chuck had talked about football and ice fishing and snowmobiling. Or maybe it was because he was good-natured and clearly harmless. And really, what man didn't like to see other men admiring their woman? As long as it was all in fun, and they knew nothing would come of it.

Just before they left, Lauren used one of the husband's phones to take a picture of all the ladies with Chuck in the middle. And then a picture of Chuck with each one of the women, his arm around their backs. Big smiles on all the ladies' faces, and a big one on Chuck's, too.

As the last car drove off, Chuck turned that smile to her. "You ready?"

"Ready for what?"

"Ready to learn how to shoot a gun."

"I don't know if I can kill anyone." She spoke loudly, her ear protection on.

Chuck leaned forward and shouted back at her. "What if they wanted to take out Falco?"

She stared at him. In her belly, anger churned. Without another word, she snapped around, held on to the pistol, not shooting right away—her finger not even on the trigger, because Chuck had told her about five times not to do so until she was about to shoot. Besides, she didn't want to accidentally shoot herself in the foot. And before doing anything, she needed to go over everything he'd said, letting it all sink into her mind.

Only then did she lift the pistol with her right hand. Leaning forward, she used her left hand to steady the gun, then took a deep breath and drew the trigger toward her. The kick lashed through her hand to her arm to the side of her chest and the back of her spine.

Clamping her teeth together, she shot again.

And again.

She pictured her husband, the man who was causing all her problems, in the target. She didn't know if Paul was dead or not. She suspected so, only because he hadn't touched his bank accounts. But maybe that had been his plan to trick her or anyone else into believing he was dead. It was possible that he'd cheated the insurance companies he was connected with. Or his clients.

Or it could be that someone *had* killed Paul.

The thought didn't bring her grief.

Nor did it bring her satisfaction.

She felt nothing for him. Thoughts of him just made her feel tired and empty—and pissed off that his actions might have put her life in danger. And not just hers but Falco's, too, and everyone who befriended her.

Somehow all of this was connected to him.

So she shot, imaging every shot hitting Paul as one kick after another went through her arm, until the fifth time, because Chuck had only let her put five bullets in the gun.

"Let's see how you did," Chuck said, and the target rolled down to them.

She kept her ear protectors on, and she was shaking inside and breathing too fast. That had been...oddly exhilarating. Every shot had been a jolt of power.

"Well, fuck," Chuck said. "You sure this is your first time? I've seen pros who haven't done as well."

She stared at the outline. Only one bullet was outside the outline of the head, and two were in the middle, just a space away from the other.

If the target had been a real man, he'd be dead.

"I guess I needed the right motivation," she said.

"That's what my mom always tells me," Chuck said. "You want to share your motivation?"

She handed him the gun, because she didn't know what to do with it, and now she was starting to feel shaky. "My motivation is that someone tried to kill me."

"Don't worry about it in my house." Chuck's jaw tightened, and his eyes squinted as if he were looking down the barrel of a rifle.

She shivered. She hadn't known he could look like that.

Looking so vengeful, he was actually...well, *hot.*

Still not her type, but sometimes who cared about type? Besides, she was pretty sure that an uptight, too-thin woman who was on someone's hit list wouldn't be on his *to-do* list.

But if she did give him the right signals, she was also pretty sure he would make an exception.

And why not give him the signals? The shy smile, the slight shoulder lift, the softening of her eyes and her lips... She knew the body language that women gave men to show they were interested, though she normally eschewed them. After all, she wasn't that kind of a woman.

But why not be that woman? After all, she might be murdered any day. The hell with being so tight-assed.

And he was looking at her now, his expression changed, the look a man had when he saw someone he admired.

Her skin heated. Why not try it for once? Why not not do him? Why hold back?

An image popped into her mind. *Adam.* Immediately she cooled, the desire gone as if she'd snapped her fingers and uttered the magic word.

She stepped back as his mouth twisted with rue, his face relaxed, the tension gone.

In a second of time, with just one look, message sent, message received.

"We should do another round," he said. "I think you're a natural, but it might have been a fluke."

She nodded. Maybe the blowing up of her house might have been a fluke, too, and nothing to do with her or Paul. Maybe she should just relax and not worry. Think positively and not question everything.

But the last time she'd decided to not question everything, she'd married Paul. From now on, she was going to prepare for the worst.

Another round sounded like a good idea.

Thirty-four

Sometimes you have to love. Other times you have to kill. ~Pooka

In the front office as usual, Darryl stared down at the small notice in the back of yesterday's paper.

He should have left it at home. He must have read it about a dozen times. As if it were some kind of a maze, and if he looked at it enough, his brain would magically see a way out.

His hands holding the paper shook, because there was no magic trail out of this mess of theirs. Piper, their mom's unpaid caretaker, had looked up the law. Lauren needed to put a notice in the newspaper once a week for three weeks. After the third one, Lauren's lawyer would put through the paperwork for a divorce. Unless Paul suddenly popped up, it would be granted. And there was nothing Darryl could do about it.

Well, just *one* thing. But he wouldn't do it. He couldn't do it. Even though it would solve all their problems.

Piper knew it, too.

He'd promised her that somehow they would get through this.

She hadn't believed him.

It wasn't her fault. It wasn't anyone's fault.

She was on the edge of hysteria. Scared.

They were all just scared.

Their lives had been hard for what seemed like forever, though he remembered an easier time, before his father left. And then there was a bad stretch, but his mother remarried, and things had been better for a while.

But one day his stepfather's job was gone. Six months later, he was out of the picture, and there was only him, his mother, and Piper. By then his mother had gained so much weight, and she had a hard time getting up the stairs, and Piper was doing the shopping, and they were barely getting by on the money he made.

And Piper...she had no life, staying home to take care of their mother.

And now their lives were falling apart, about to go into flames.

When that happened, there sometimes seemed only one thing they could do.

Only one thing *she* would do.

But it was wrong, so wrong. And he didn't know how to stop her. Except for two ways.

And one of them was murder...

Thirty-five

Sometimes the eyes tell the story.
~Pooka

It was less than three weeks before Christmas, and nearly every home Adam drove past was decorated. Stores that weren't closed for the winter were brightly lit. Even some tourists were coming back for the holidays, ready to celebrate in the country wonderland.

People were happy.

His daughter was happy.

And he wanted to say two words: *Bah, humbug.*

He drove into the driveway of Sylvia's bed-and-breakfast. Instead of going to the front door, he went around to the back door. Falco was in the yard, and he rushed up to Adam to sniff and greet him. Adam rang the doorbell, and Lauren opened it. The tip of her nose was pink, as if she'd recently rushed from her car in the small parking area to the kitchen. She greeted him politely, but then she looked down and at Falco and asked, "Did you go potty?"

Falco's answer was in his big smile, and she let him come in and then Adam, heading into the kitchen.

Adam's mood lightened. "I went potty, too."

She turned and socked his arm.

He kissed her. Hard, fast, as if it were something he needed badly.

He was becoming addicted to her kisses.

He stepped back. "You put the notice in the paper."

She pressed her lips together. She was wearing her work clothes. A pale pink sweater that showed off her small, rounded breasts, and gray wool-looking slacks that skimmed her hips and her long legs. Nothing about her was flashy. Except for her face, neck, and hands, there was no skin showing. But none of that stopped him from imagining what she looked like without the clothes. After all, he'd seen her naked. He'd seen her with her eyes hot with passion.

Something about her today was just so...enticing.

Something about her every day.

Then Chuck wandered into the kitchen, his jawline scruffy, his jeans old, and he wore a sweatshirt that said, *No Way*. Chuck greeted him, then poured a mug of coffee, asking Adam if he wanted some. When he said no, Chuck leaned his butt against the kitchen counter, the corners of his mouth turned up. Holding his mug, Chuck watched him and Lauren as if they were his amusement.

Adam wore jeans and a sweatshirt, too, and his jaw was also scruffy. Hell, he'd been outside most of the day, working on a foundation for a new shopping center in the next town. Not the best weather to do this, but the best weather was when the influx of tourists began, so they had to do what they could when they could.

That was his life. Doing what needed to be done.

As he thought that, a howl roared up inside him. He wanted more in his life. He wanted Lauren.

And he wanted her alive.

"Yes, I put the notice in," she said finally. "I need to in order to divorce Paul. This whole thing is a process, but it should be over next month."

He stepped closer to her, stopping less than two feet away. "Isn't there a different way you can do this? A more private way? I can't forget that someone tried to kill you."

"We don't know for sure that anyone tried to kill me. It might have been kids playing with explosives. Or someone who chose my house at random."

"Yeah," Chuck said. "Crazy people are all around us."

Adam glared at Chuck, who grinned at him, then grabbed an apple off of the counter, not at all fazed. Adam turned back to Lauren. Her elbows were askew, her hands on her hips, her hard stare letting him know that nothing he said was going to stop her from doing what she had to do.

"You should stay with me." The words blurted out of his mouth.

Her jaw dropped, her mouth opened, her eyes wide.

A crunch came from his left. Chuck chomping into the apple.

Didn't he have better things to do? Couldn't Chuck see that he wanted a few private moments with Lauren?

"I'm worried." Adam lowered his voice. "We've known each other a long time. If anything happened to you..." He inhaled shakily.

She sucked in her lower lip, her forehead creasing. For a second, he thought she was going to lean forward and put her arms around his back. Lay the side of her head against his chest.

The vision was so bright and perfect and real that he held his breath in. Waiting for it to happen.

Instead, her arms rose up. Not to hold him against her but to splay her hands on his chest and hold him off. "If someone wants to blow me up, I can't take the chance they would hurt you or Tori. You understand that, don't you? You don't want to take the chance that Tori would be hurt."

He closed his eyes, because she had him there.

This was hell seven times over.

"We have alarms with cameras and motion sensors," Chuck said. "You don't have to worry about leaving Lauren here. I'll take care of her."

"I haven't given anyone my new address, either." Lauren shrugged. "Except for work and the sheriff's office."

"What about your husband's friends?"

She shook her head, though there was a frown on her forehead. He wasn't an expert on body language, but that frown told him something.

"What?" he asked, folding his arms.

"I did tell my stepson."

Out of the corner of his eye, Chuck shook his head.

Fuck, Adam thought. *Just fuck.*

"Rodney would never hurt me," Lauren said. "He likes me. He knows I don't want his father's money. He knows it's going to him."

"Maybe he doesn't care about his father's money," Chuck said.

Adam glanced at him, then back to Lauren. "Chuck's right. Maybe he cares about losing *your* money."

"I'm alive! Besides, I'm helping him through college."

"You're alive now." Adam leaned forward so that his head was tilting a few inches over her. Intimidation, but damn it, someone needed to intimidate a sense of safety into her head. "But if you die before the divorce—"

"Or if she's murdered," Chuck said.

"Wisconsin is a community property state," she said. "But I inherited funds from my grandparents before I married Paul. It will not automatically go to Rodney."

"Who is the money going to?" Adam shook his head. "No, I shouldn't ask that."

"Charities, for the most part. Some for Rodney." She looked into his eyes and held his gaze. "And some will go to Tori."

His heart missed a beat, then beat faster. "I can take care of my daughter." He held out his hand before she could tell him how much a college education cost. As if he didn't know that his daughter would have to take out loans. That he would help her out as much as he could. That there would be medical bills, too, unless someone found a cure for type one diabetes in the next six years. "But that's not the problem."

It was her turn to fold her arms. "What is?"

"That you're still officially married," Chuck said before Adam could say anything. "If you die and your husband turns up, he might get your money. Or he might think he will. Either way, you'll be dead."

Adam's eyebrows shot up. Chuck wasn't known for his smarts, but now and then, he came out with these zingers.

"If he's not already dead," she whispered.

Adam nodded, and she closed her eyes. He wanted to pull her against him, but there was Chuck in the room, and—

He drew her to his chest. The hell with Chuck watching them.

Her arms slowly curved around his back. His hands crossed behind her back. "I'm afraid for you," he murmured.

She lifted her head. "Me, too."

There was a sound from behind him. Chuck stepping away from the counter. "I'm picking up a meal from the diner," he said. "I probably won't be back for an hour or so. If you need me sooner, call me. I can pick up something for you, too."

His footsteps thumped on the floor. Adam kept holding Lauren, his head down, his cheek and jaw against her silken hair. She kept clinging to him while Chuck opened the coat closet in the back, then put on his jacket before the closet door thumped shut. A moment later, the back door opened and then closed.

Leaving just them.

They still didn't move. Not until they heard a car start and then drive away.

Adam lifted his head. "I'm sorry."

"What for?" Her lips curved up slightly, but her eyes...they looked sad. And gentle. And vulnerable.

"Let's go to your room," he said.

She didn't say anything. Instead, she turned and held out her hand behind her. He took it and let her lead him upstairs, following her like males had been following women since the Homo erectus species showed up. Maybe even before that.

All he knew was that he wanted to follow her everywhere. Anywhere.

Especially to her room on the third floor.

Thirty-six

Sex fogs up the brain. But sometimes a little fog is good for the grass and the air. And sometimes a little sex is good for the human. ~Pooka

Next to Lauren, Adam was sleeping on the bed, wiped out, his mouth open but no snores coming out, just husky breaths that seemed to come from the bottom of his lungs.

Lauren stared at the ceiling, not wanting to move. They'd done a lot of deep breathing during the last half hour. Wonderful deep breaths.

And wonderful deep plunges, moans and groans, touching and kissing, and holding on and more primal sounds coming from them. She'd screamed. Muffled screams, but still screams, holding on to him tightly. She was pretty sure she'd left fingernail imprints in the skin over his biceps.

She'd closed the door before the lovemaking, keeping Falco in the hall, which had been smart. He might have thought they were hurting each other, and though he was a gentle giant, he would have tried to protect her. Instead, he'd growled a few times on the other side of the door. She'd felt sorry for him, but just for a few seconds. Too busy hanging onto Adam and calling out, "Oh, my God! Don't stop! Don't stop!"

His phone rang.

She rolled off of the bed, where he lay on his back, his legs open, his arms at his side, his face relaxed. This was the first time she'd seen his face relaxed since...well, the last time they'd had sex, but that hadn't lasted long.

Another ring, and she grabbed the phone, looked at the name, and made a face. Not because she didn't like the person on the other end. She liked the person very well. She *loved* her. The air was cool on her body, but she put the phone to her ear. She needed to answer this now.

"Hi, Tori. Your dad's here, but he's, um, in the bathroom."

He moaned, and she looked behind her, but his eyes were closed. The condom he'd used was still on his penis, and right now it looked saggy and sad.

She didn't feel sad. She felt like doing it again. Soon. Very soon.

"I'm home," Tori said. "I wondered where he was."

His eyes opened, and he held out his hand.

"Just a minute." She handed the phone to him, then headed to the bathroom.

When she came back, he was off the phone, in his jeans and T-shirt already, pulling on a sweatshirt. His head popped out, and he said, "You're invited for dinner."

"You know I can't." She grabbed her housecoat out of the closet and put it on before turning back to him.

"No one knows you'll be there. Have dinner with us and stay awhile."

She stared at him. "Don't tempt me."

He stared back. "Come home with me. Tori misses you. I think even the pooka is missing you."

"Bullshit."

He smiled, the skin at the outer corners of his eyes crinkling. He looked so handsome and so loving. And she did want to be with him. He was right. It wasn't likely that anyone would be following her. Although...

"What is it?" he asked.

"I'm wondering how hard it would be to sneak Falco into your car. So no one would know we were going with you."

The hand he held out didn't waver. "I know just about every car in the area. If there's a stranger's car, I'll spot it."

She shook her head. "What if the person who blew up my house is someone we know?"

"I'll spot that, too." Then he took her hand and pulled her to him and kissed her.

Sometime during that kiss, she decided that he was right.

This time.

But she wasn't going to make a habit of it. Not until her divorce was final.

And she was taking her gun with her. She'd

been to the indoor shooting range about three times since Chuck had taken her the first time. She'd already bought a Glock for her own use. The shooting range owner said she was a natural.

She didn't want to kill anyone, but if someone tried to kill her, her dog, or her friends, she would shoot to kill.

It was just the practical thing to do.

Thirty-seven

Love makes you happier than hate.
~Pooka

"Are you going to be here for Christmas?" Tori plopped her butt down on the foot of her bed, the mattress springing up and down.

Pooka opened one icy blue eye. "Do you have to bounce?"

Tori giggled and gave another bounce. "Bouncing is fun."

Pooka sighed. "Teenagers."

Tori giggled again. School had been good, except for algebra. In her English class, they'd talked about the *nemesis*. The bad guy. Like Voldemort in Harry Potter books. Or the Wicked Witch in *The Wizard of Oz*. Her nemesis wasn't a person; it was algebra.

What did anyone need algebra for? She'd rather stick pins into her arms than sit through another algebra class. It was forcing her brain into paths where her brain didn't want to go. She didn't know what algebra was good for, but it for sure wasn't good for her A average in every other subject.

Maybe her extracurricular activities would help make up the difference. She wrapped her arms around herself and giggled.

"Something good happened," Pooka said.

"I was going to tell my dad first." She had her legs crossed and rocked back and forth.

"All right." Pooka closed her eyes and settled down to sleep.

"If you really want me to tell you..." Tori unwrapped her arms and uncrossed her legs and turned around to face Pooka, then crossed her legs again. "You'll never guess what happened."

"In that case, you had better tell me."

"I talked to the whole school today." Her voice rose, and she didn't care. "I talked about diabetes. I wasn't supposed to, but the nurse who was going to talk about flu shots couldn't make it. They were going to cancel it, but the principal decided to ask me and Alex to talk." She leaned forward and stared into Pooka's blue eyes. "Alex is in fifth grade, and he has Down's syndrome. He has a round head and he likes cats and dogs."

"Is that all?" Pooka yawned, showing her sharp teeth.

"He said his mom told him if he's nice to people and smiles a lot, the other kids will like him. And then he smiled at everyone."

"Did it work?"

"I don't know if *everyone* likes him, but I do."

A paw patted her knee. "The boy's mother must be very smart. And so is he."

"I agree." Tori beamed at Pooka. "Some of the girls cried a little."

"Boys cry, too," Pooka said. "They just hide it better."

"Maybe. He didn't talk too long, but everyone clapped for him. And then it was my turn. At first my voice shook, but I remembered something that my mom had told me when I was giving a book report in second grade. She said, 'Just pretend that you're telling *me* about it.' So that's what I did. I pictured her sitting in the auditorium. And you know what?"

Pooka stared, not saying anything. But she didn't put her head down and close her eyes, so Tori took that to mean she was interested. "Everything got better. I pretended I was practicing with her, and it all just kind of flowed out. Easy. Except for one thing." She leaned forward. "Not telling them about you."

A door slammed downstairs. Her dad. She scrambled off the bed, heading toward the hallway. Before she reached it, she turned around. "Why don't you come down and see my dad? You're part of the family."

"No, I'm not," Pooka said.

"If you're not part of the family, then why are you here?"

"I don't know yet, but there's a reason. When I know, we'll all know."

Tori gave a long sigh. "Are all pookas as enigmatic as you?"

"Enigmatic? That's a big word."

"I'm smarter with words than algebra. Are you trying to avoid answering me?"

"See? You are smart."

Tori frowned. "This is something about Lauren, isn't it? Is someone going to try to kill her again? And how come you're here and not with her?"

"I don't know." Pooka let out a hiss of displeasure, and Tori could tell that she didn't like not knowing.

"Is this because God works in mysterious ways?" Tori asked.

"No, it's because people work in stupid ways."

Tori giggled, then hurried into the hall and down the stairs. She wished she could've told the whole school about Pooka, but if she had, they would've just thought she was nuts.

She hoped nothing would happen soon, to Lauren or to her or her dad. She didn't want any of them to get hurt. And she didn't want Pooka to go away, either. Though Pooka took up more than half her bed and stayed upstairs all the time, Tori loved her. Love didn't care about things like that. Love just cared about love.

Thirty-eight

When you take a step, you leave a footprint. Even if you can't see it, there are always consequences. ~Pooka

It was Saturday morning, ten days before Christmas, and Lauren woke up with an idea. A big one.

The idea stuck to her as she threw on her housecoat and hurried downstairs to put Falco out in the back, hooking him up to a rope that Chuck had put together. While he did his thing, she rushed back to the third floor and showered and then dressed quickly. She left her bed unmade for now, something she didn't like to do, but Falco was more important than a made-up bed.

Before she reached the first floor, she could smell the coffee. It was calling her name. When she stepped into the kitchen, Falco was already eating out of his big bowl in the corner. Chuck was yawning and pouring coffee into his mug.

Chuck greeted her in the middle of a yawn, his

blond hair tousled and his unshaven face good-looking enough to be on a magazine cover. "Scrambled eggs again? Or over easy? I made blueberry muffins, too."

She leaned against the counter. "So many choices. You'd make a wonderful husband."

"I would. Too bad you have another candidate in mind."

Her face heated, and Chuck grinned. Of course he grinned. He'd been home almost every time Adam was able to sneak away last week. Sometimes only an hour—but they were quality hours.

Chuck raised his right hand. "Don't worry about it getting around. What happens in my *casa* stays in my *casa*."

She still felt embarrassed. Having booty calls wasn't something she did every day. Even every year. But she wasn't complaining. And she wasn't going to stop.

"Of course," Chuck continued, "you know that almost everyone in town has seen the truck parked in front and has come to the same conclusion."

"No!" She had a sinking feeling in her belly. "Do you think Tori knows?"

"I don't know. She's what? Eleven?"

"Twelve, almost thirteen. She's in sixth grade."

"Well, the grown-ups might be careful what they say around her or the other kids. I'd say you're safe."

She sighed. She'd have to tell Adam.

"Sorry about that," Chuck said. "You looked so happy when you came into the kitchen, too. I think you were skipping."

"I might have danced a little. I had an idea."

"Yeah?" He poured coffee into another mug and handed it to her. "Spill. And I don't mean the coffee."

She took the mug, looking straight at him. "Are you doing anything special for Christmas?"

"Besides eating too much and then groaning about all that I ate? Not really. What about you? Didn't you say December is the busiest month for nonprofit fundraisers?"

"It is, but after nearly nine years at the hospital, I have it fairly well nailed. My list's all set, plus the extra names that Ashleigh and I added this year."

"Ashleigh?"

"My assistant." She narrowed her eyes at him. "She's married, but she has a sister about two years younger than you. You would love her."

"Oh, no. No fixing me up." He held up his left hand as if warding her off. "Though if you decide to get rid of that old guy you're seeing, you know where to find me."

She laughed, shaking her head.

"Why is this time of year so busy?" he asked. "You'd think you'd have the rest of the year off."

"Most people think so, but it's actually the opposite." She gave him a crooked smile. "This is the last month donors can make charitable contributions and deduct them from their taxes."

"You're kidding?"

"There's no kidding in fundraising. It's a war out there."

"Who wins?"

"The one who gets the most money."

"You?"

"We don't do badly. This had been one of my best years. And Ashleigh is amazing. We already have the emails scheduled for the last three days of the year, reminding donors and potential donors of the tax deduction benefits, letting them know how their money will benefit patients and families of patients. Reminding them of the desperate need, especially for the outreach help for veterans and children."

"With pictures that will tear at the heartstrings," Chuck said. "And their wallets."

"Absolutely. Ashleigh is so good at getting these pictures. We send out letters, too. I'll print one and bring it to you. You pay taxes, right? May as well give it to us instead of the government. Who knows what they'll spend it on? Probably something you don't like. And this is going to needy people in our community."

He looked at her admiringly. "You are good."

She laughed. "Seriously, it's a great way to end the year, giving to people who need it. Do you want to send it to the hospital to help veterans, cancer patients, and needy families? Or do you want to send it to the government to pay for programs you don't agree with?"

"You actually say that?"

"Of course not. We say *around* it."

"You should be a politician."

She made a face. Just what she *didn't* need to do now that her love life was amazing. Wonderful. Her Christmas gift to herself.

She felt like the flighty teenager she'd never been. Carefree and sexy. Thinking with her heart—and her vagina—instead of her brain.

It wouldn't last. Even in the midst of her euphoria, a darkness hovered in her mind. A sense that something was going to happen. And when it did, it was going to be bad.

The fear and the urgency made her treasure each encounter with Adam. She'd had more orgasms in these few weeks than she'd had with Paul during their years of marriage before he'd disappeared.

Maybe that's what had given her the idea to host a Christmas dinner. Her parents were agnostics—they thought an afterlife was possible but weren't sure about the "one God thing." They certainly wouldn't celebrate a holiday dedicated to a fat man in a red suit who gave candy and presents to kids. And this year, Adam's parents were driving to the Upper Peninsula in Michigan to have Christmas with his grandparents on his dad's side.

Lauren suspected that Adam and Tori were staying in Trouble Bay to keep her company, though Adam insisted it was because of Pooka, which made her laugh. Maybe it *was* Pooka...or maybe it was her.

The bed-and-breakfast wasn't her home, but it felt more like one with its big kitchen than her home that she and Paul had decorated in neutral colors and modern lines. So perfect and so cold. A one-hundred-eighty-degree difference from the warmth and welcome atmosphere of the bed-and-breakfast.

Maybe she felt that way because of her trysts with Adam. It was just a temporary place, and in the spring, her home would be rebuilt. But for now, she was happy here.

For now, she wanted to do this.

"I don't know if you're having any guests at Christmas," she said, "but—"

"No guests," Chuck said, and opened his mouth to add something, but she jumped in.

"Good. I'd like to invite Adam and Tori. I'll make ham and pies and vegetables." She stood in the kitchen very straight, even as she wondered if all that great sex had melted her brain. She wasn't really a good cook. She could follow directions, but cooking wasn't joyful for her. Possibly because she normally cooked for herself. As a result, she made a lot of salads and soups and protein shakes. Healthy and quick.

But a sense of urgency was driving her to do this. The same urgency she wanted the hospital donors to feel. As if it were their last chance to give.

Because this might really be her last chance.

And her first. Which made it her first and last.

Or *going out with a big bang.*

Like the explosion at her house. She'd called Sergeant Nichols earlier this week. He'd said because nothing else had happened, the explosion might have been a fluke. Probably a couple teens doing something stupid that scared the hell out of them, and they would never do it again.

She wanted him to be right, but her instincts told her that he was wrong.

"Didn't I tell you?" Chuck asked.

She frowned, giving him her attention, grateful to change her thread of thoughts.

"My mom will be home for Christmas," he said. "She wasn't planning on it, but she changed her mind. She won't be alone, either."

"Oh." Lauren stepped back. She didn't know why she hadn't thought of this before. Of course, Sylvia would want to have Christmas with her son. "I suppose you're inviting someone, too."

"Not for Christmas. I'm saving Christmas for someone special." He winked at her. "I was going to invite you, though two more guests will be just about right."

"I couldn't—"

"My mom always makes a ton of food for Christmas. She prefers turkey over ham, and the turkey isn't the only one who gets stuffed. We all do. I'm glad I don't have to climb up any steps after eating. Don't think I could make it. I swear, you'd think she's cooking for twelve instead of just a few."

"I couldn't—"

"She was moaning on the phone because she was late making up her mind, and her friends here had already made other plans. She asked if you were doing anything."

"I can't invite people without her okay."

His phone was on the table. He pulled it in front of him and started texting. He set it aside. "Done." There was a smug look on his face.

Before she could say anything, his phone buzzed. He grabbed it, looking at the display. He turned to her. "It's a go. Invite Adam and his daughter." His eyebrows rose. "And aren't you glad you don't have to stuff the turkey?"

She laughed. He was right. She was glad.

"Thank her, please. Tell her I'll make an apple pie."

She got the time from him, then he said, "This is the first year that my mom isn't opening the inn for Christmas. I almost can't believe it, but good for her."

"Good for her," Lauren said, but her voice was faint. "You're sure she doesn't mind me being here?" Next to her, Falco woofed. She patted his head. "And my dog?"

"If she minded, she would've said so. My mom doesn't have a problem saying no."

She thanked him, then took her coffee to the living room, where she phoned Adam while Falco lay down next to her chair.

Adam answered and agreed to Christmas at the bed-and-breakfast.

As soon as she hung up, the phone rang. She picked it up and saw Darryl's name on the display. She sighed and put it to her ear. "Hello, Darryl."

"Hello. You didn't call this month yet."

"I won't be calling every month from now on." She heard her voice a little sharp, and took a deep breath. "I thought I made it clear last month. I've been a little busy lately, and you know more about the business than I do. I trust you."

"Um...I...um..."

"Is there anything in particular you wanted to tell me?" she asked.

"Well, I saw the notice in the paper. You really are divorcing Paul."

"That's the plan." She grimaced. None of this was his fault. He was a nice guy. She knew that Paul had taken advantage of him, and she shouldn't take her irritation out on him. "If you want to buy the agency, that's certainly something we could work out. Send me a proposal. I'll talk to Wendy and see what we can do."

There was silence. "When do you need it by?"

"I'm busy at the office until Christmas."

"So am I. What about Christmas day? I can come to your place on Christmas day."

"I have plans for Christmas day."

"At the bed-and-breakfast?"

She frowned. "Excuse me?"

"You're right. I'm sorry. I didn't mean... I would never... I'll, um, put the proposal together and call you after Christmas. Good-bye."

She hung up. That was odd, though she'd always thought Darryl was a bit odd. But many people she knew were odd. Including herself. And she couldn't remember telling him where she was staying, but Paul's agency had clients in Trouble Bay, and one of them might have mentioned her temporary residence. As much as she wanted to keep it quiet, that just didn't work in a small town like this. If there was a favorite entertainment in Trouble Bay, it was neighbors talking about neighbors.

She stepped to the front window and looked out at the winter wonderland, immediately feeling calmer. A blanket of snow covered the grass and the tree branches sparkled with snow crystals, too. The sky was pale blue with fluffy clouds. Across Main Street, the stores were decorated, and the street looked festive, like an old-fashioned Christmas.

Something bumped against her hip. Falco's head. She put her hand on his head and scratched his ear. "We're going to have a wonderful Christmas, Falco."

And after that?

A chill went through her, because there was always an *after* for her. And never had it started with *happily*.

Maybe this time, she thought, and she stepped back from the window. Walking away, she told herself that this Christmas would be good.

Falco whined and she hunkered down, put her arms around him, and hugged him. Inside her chest, her heart thundered as she repeated in her mind, *It will be good. It will, it will, it will.*

Thirty-nine

The humans are getting ready for a feast. I'm getting ready for trouble.
~Pooka

"You sure they don't mind if I come?" Josh asked as he and Tori waited on the concrete stoop in front of Tori's house for her dad to pull the car out of the garage.

Tori rolled her eyes. He'd asked the same question at least five times. "Yes. I called, and Sylvia said she had plenty of food."

"You call her Sylvia?" His eyebrows went way up.

She flipped her hair back, and for once, she felt like one of the cool girls. Though being able to call Sylvia by her name really wasn't that cool. "Sylvia was kind of a friend of my mom's and my grandma's. They called her Sylvia, so I did, too, when I was little."

"Doesn't she mind?"

"Why should she? It's her name."

"Yeah, but she..." He shook his head. "Never mind."

She put her lips together and didn't push it. He probably felt embarrassed that his mom was with her boyfriend and had planned on leaving him alone on Christmas.

It made her want to cry, but she blinked away the moisture in her eyes, and then she had to clear her throat before speaking. "I know what you mean. She's kind of like royalty. But Lauren's staying at her place, and she likes her. Plus, Sylvia's fine with us going over there, so we may as well enjoy it."

"Know what I just realized?" Josh asked. "Thinking about Sylvia?"

She shook her head.

"I realized that if someone feels intimidating to me, it's because they have more confidence than I do."

She stared at him, and he frowned, his lips parted. The bottom lip was full, and it looked soft. She wondered what it would feel like to kiss him. She'd never kissed a boy yet. "That's pretty smart of you," she said.

He grinned. Apparently he liked being called smart.

A car beeped. Her dad.

"We'd better go." Josh reached for her mittened hand with his gloved hand. But before he could grab it, he pulled his hand back, looking surprised. As if his hand had done it without his permission.

He liked her! He did!

She ran to the car, smiling widely. Life was super-cool today.

Forty

Showtime!
~Pooka

Pooka knew about time. Knew it only took about five minutes to get to the place where Lauren was staying. Pooka also knew about eternity. But it was *cold* standing in front of the bed-and-breakfast, waiting for Tori and her dad and the boy. Five minutes in this frigid weather was starting to feel like an eternity.

Once, a long time ago, when the earth was much younger, she had experienced cold. But some things were better forgotten.

Then there was the white stuff covering the grass but not the sidewalks. Snow. She had often peered through windows and admired the newly fallen snow. Like a layer of whipped cream on top of a cake.

Now she knew that, in truth, the beauty of snow was a treacherous way to trick the unwary. She had stepped in it, and there was nothing sweet about snow. It was just plain *cold*.

Why was it taking them so long? Were they pushing the car?

Other cars were driving slowly down the road. Very slowly. None of them belonged to Pooka's people.

Then she saw it. Not the truck that Adam normally drove but the car with Tori and Josh in the back seat. *Finally.*

They parked in the driveway. Pooka rushed to the side and slid to a stop, her gaze on the packed-down snow. There was no other choice. She would have to step on the snow.

Hissing, she sped over the snow as the others trooped to the door in the back, all of them carrying something. As Adam poked the doorbell, a chime resounded. In her shrunken body, Pooka scolded them with her feline voice.

They stared at her.

"What's that?" Josh asked.

She scolded louder. She could talk better English than any of them, but humans were unpredictable, and she didn't know what they would do if, in this small cat form, she talked to them in their language.

She raised her voice instead and directed her scolding to Tori.

"Whatever it is," Josh said, "it's trying to tell you something."

Still holding a bag, Tori bent her knees. In a hushed tone, she said, "I think it's Pooka."

"Tori." Adam's voice was sharp like a knife, and there was a frown on his forehead. "That's impossible."

Stupid humans. They didn't know that, for a pooka, *everything* was possible.

The door opened, and a woman with hair the color of a pale sun greeted them.

Adam said something to her, and as she did, Pooka ran in front of Adam and zipped around the woman's feet, thinking, *Stop me if you can.*

Of course she knew they wouldn't be able to stop her.

She had a job to do, the reason she'd been sent here. She'd had enough naps. Now it was time for action. And she wasn't going to let any humans get in her way.

Forty-one

Dinners should never be interrupted. It's just rude. ~Pooka

Adam narrowed his eyes. Chuck had taken their bags and their jackets. They were all in the kitchen now, along with the uninvited kitten.

The cat hissed at Falco, and the big dog backed away. Lauren put her hand on Falco's head. Was he bowing his head? No, just turning it to the side, as if wondering what this small, hissing creature was.

"Looks like David and Goliath." Chuck returned, an amused tilt on his lips. "David won that fight. If I were you, I'd take the cat home." He looked straight at Adam.

"It's not my cat," he said.

"We found it as we got out of the car," Josh said.

Tori knelt, holding her hand out to the cat, which rubbed its mouth on the side of her hand. "No, it found us."

Adam stiffened. It had seemed to him that the

cat was waiting for him to park the car and get out. Waiting to claim them.

"Pooka?" Tori asked in a soft voice.

The cat purred and rubbed its mouth on her again.

Then it looked at Adam, and he saw its eyes. Ice blue. He'd seen cats with eyes that were blue, but never a cat eyes like this.

Tori had, though. He could hear her voice in his head. *The pooka has eyes like ice over Lake Michigan. And her fur is like black velvet.*

He felt cold. Colder now than when he'd been outside in the below-freezing temperature.

"It ran in ahead of us, and we thought it belonged here." Josh walked over to Sylvia, pulling out a box of chocolates from his bag. "This is for you."

She smiled graciously. "Why, thank you. This is lovely."

His complexion reddened. He mumbled something.

A hand touched Adam's arm. Lauren.

Seeing her, Adam breathed easier. Almost as if the world had been tilted wrong, and one look at her tilted it back to the right place.

"Josh is a great kid," Lauren said.

Adam nodded, glad to talk to her. And certainly glad to talk about anything other than the cat. "He deserves better than a mother who neglects him and a father he's never known."

"He's got you and Tori now," she said in a low voice. "You're part of his family, the way Noelle was part of mine."

He stared at her face that was soft with

compassion, and he wished they were alone.

"I have a funny feeling about today," she said.

"Good or bad?"

"Both."

He frowned. He didn't believe in intuition.

But neither did he believe in pookas.

"Good," he said. "It's all going to be good. Except for the cat. Someone might be looking for it."

"I think you're right," Sylvia said. "Though I can't think of anyone who has a black cat."

"Is it okay if it stays here?" Tori raised her imploring gaze to Sylvia. "Please? It's freezing out, and it's so small and thin. I'm afraid it will die."

Adam's lips twisted. Very melodramatic. Now Tori was giving Sylvia her *poor, little motherless child* look.

He should be angry at Tori, but instead he was proud.

Chuck laughed before his mother could say anything. "We have a couple bags of kitty litter in the garage. We've been using it to keep the driveway from icing up. Mom, can you find me a box? I'll pour some kitty litter in it. We can put it in the back hall." He looked at Tori. "Does he have a name?"

"I don't know." Tori's eyes were big. "It's not my cat, but I think it's a girl."

"If it's not your cat, then how do you know it's a girl?"

"She let me pet her belly, showing me her under-body. I'm twelve. I know about penises, and she doesn't have one."

Adam groaned as Josh's face turned red, and

the others choked on a laugh. Then Chuck went to put litter in the box for the cat, and Sylvia pushed the others into the living room, insisting she would take care of everything. They would just get in the way.

As they headed there, the cat went first.

Adam had the odd sense that the cat was checking it out for danger.

This wasn't like him. He shook his head and turned to Lauren to admire her perfect nose and her perfect ears. She wore pearl earrings and a red sweater.

"This is the first time I've seen you in red," he said, slowing so they lagged behind the others. "You look beautiful."

"It's Christmas. And all good things should happen today."

"Do you believe that?"

She smiled, but it was a sad smile. "I believe it *should* happen."

"It should," he said as they followed the others into the living room. As he did, he looked around, and then he saw that Lauren was doing the same thing. Looking around. Only in her case, it seemed to him as if she were looking for enemies.

The hair on the back of his neck rose.

And so did the cat's.

Forty-two

Houses can feel like heaven, especially when the food is good. ~Pooka

They were barely settling into the living room when a gray-haired man walked in. Lauren had met Nate, Sylvia's professor boyfriend, yesterday. He wore black-rimmed glasses below his bushy eyebrows and above his bulbous nose, and a sweatshirt that said *I'm Sylvia's Friend in Low Places*. In addition to what he called "my college gig," he wrote screenplays and had a sharp sense of humor. Not the typical Door County resident, though there were a lot of artists in the county. Besides, Lauren didn't think any of the locals thought of themselves as typical.

Adam set down a small gift bag on the coffee table, then he shook Nate's hand. "You probably don't remember me, but we met during the summer."

"The best summer of my life." Nate looked in the direction of the kitchen, and his eyes beneath the glasses seemed to grow soft.

Watching him, Lauren felt a little soft, too. She hadn't met him last year, but she'd heard about the odd pairing of Sylvia and the professor. There had been less gossip than normal, though, because their romance had started about the same time as the unsolved Fourth of July murder.

Her teeth clenched. If something like that could happen on a summer holiday, in public, while the town's dignitaries were making celebratory speeches, it could happen again at Christmas.

Lauren had woken this morning with her stomach tense, and that hadn't changed. She didn't know where the tension came from, but she glanced at her purse on the bookshelf in the corner. The purse without her loaded gun in it.

She couldn't take the chance that any of the kids might bump it and it would somehow go off.

Besides, Sylvia and Chuck were here. And so was Adam. *Nothing* was going to go wrong today.

Chuck turned on the TV, and *Miracle on 34th Street* was on. After twenty minutes, Lauren's stomach calmed, but she was still aware of tension when Chuck stepped in again. "Heads up, ladies and funny men. Dinner's almost ready." He looked at the TV. "My favorite movie. I'm missing it." With a sigh, he turned back to the kitchen.

"What are you thinking?" Adam asked.

She switched her attention to him. Just looking at him, she felt calmer. Happier. As if her stars were lining up in order. "How amazing you are."

His smile was slow. "Oh?"

She laughed softly, feeling mushy inside.

"Amazing in bed?" His grin widened.

"Of course." She grinned back. "And an amazing father."

"That's the best thing you can say about me." He put his arm around her shoulder.

She sucked her breath in and glanced at Tori.

He squeezed her arm. "I'm pretty sure she knows about us and approves." He angled to murmur in her ear. "And just so you know, amazing in bed is the second best thing."

She giggled, then forced herself to stop. *Giggling? Really?* She had *never* been a giggler.

Until today. She sat still and admitted that it was okay to giggle. Giggling meant she was having fun. Enjoying the day. The moment.

Enjoying Adam.

She laid her head on his shoulder and let her body relax. She felt calm inside now, no longer borrowing trouble. She was in love. She admitted it. And she hoped—was almost sure—that the love she felt for Adam was reciprocated.

For once, she was going to believe that everything was going to be all right.

It almost felt to her as if Noelle was looking down on them, happy for them. Blessing them.

A few minutes later, she heard the scrape of Falco getting on his feet, and she drew away from Adam.

Sylvia's beau stood. "I'll put Falco out." He put his hand on Falco's neck. "Falco and I are already best buds. Isn't that right, buddy?"

Falco looked up at Nate, his mouth open in a doggy smile.

"Let's go and let the lovebirds cuddle." As Nate headed toward the kitchen, Falco trotting behind him, Lauren put her hands over her face.

"It's okay, Lauren," Tori said. "Everyone knows. And I like it."

Lauren forced herself to put her hands down, and she smiled tentatively toward Tori and Josh, but they were already watching TV again.

"See?" Adam said, tugging her back to him. "It's all good."

She nodded. Maybe it would be good. Maybe it would be wonderful. Maybe that nagging sense that something bad was going to be happen was just fear. She wasn't used to things being so good. It felt like this day belonged to another person, not her. As if she were living Noelle's life. And even as she felt Noelle's approval, she felt guilty.

Or else maybe something bad really was going to happen.

She forced herself to relax against Adam, one muscle at a time. Taking deep breaths. Telling herself that her Miracle in Trouble Bay was starting right now.

Like Maureen O'Hara on TV, she just had to believe.

Forty-three

I smell the stench of fear.
~Pooka

Darryl was driving fast in the dimming light, snow on both sides of Highway 42. Nearly dinnertime for everyone, and the roads nearly empty. He'd left his mother home alone, but he'd had to. Once he'd read the note, he'd had no choice.

His heart was beating hard and fast, and his head felt so hot that he feared for his blood pressure. Feared the top of his head would blow off. And at the same time, feared his heart was going to burst.

He had to stop her. It was all his fault. He had to do something.

His headlights shone on a sign. *Trouble Bay.* Thank God.

Or thank the devil.

Because he couldn't see her.

He should have stopped this sooner. Heaven help him.

Heaven help them all.

Forty-four

There's a time to love, and there's a time to kick butt. ~Pooka

The movie hadn't quite ended when Sylvia stood and mentioned that dinner was about ready, but the court drama scene was over, and it was getting dark out. Lauren stood. She'd seen the movie at least a couple dozen times already, and she pictured that perfect ending in her mind. She didn't need to watch it again.

"I'll help set the table."

"Chuck can help."

"Let me do this," Lauren said. "Chuck has done plenty."

"Yeah," Chuck called out. "Chuck's done plenty. And you know this is my favorite ending."

Sylvia's face softened, and she shook her head. Lauren took that as a yes, and she headed into the kitchen. Sylvia had taken the turkey out about twenty minutes ago. Lauren rolled up her sweater sleeves and said she'd take out the stuffing.

Sylvia nodded. Lauren suspected that Sylvia thought it would keep her busy. She started to take the other food off the stove. Falco was in the kitchen, of course, paying attention to Lauren's every move. Probably hoping she would drop something.

In the hallway, the black cat was prowling. Sylvia was quiet as she worked, and Lauren suspected that she was listening to the end of the movie. They couldn't hear every word, but the happiness in the actors' voices was all that Lauren needed as she scooped out the last of the stuffing.

The back door creaked, but she was concentrating on listening to the movie dialogue, her head tilted toward the front, and she didn't pay attention. Not even when the cat hissed.

Falco barked, but she still didn't look behind her. He was a dog, and sometimes he barked. That's what dogs did.

Then the cat growled, and Lauren was done scooping out the stuffing, so she stopped to look at the cat.

The fur on its spine stood straight up

The door slammed.

"My gun," Sylvia said, her voice low as she turned toward the hallway. "Lauren, get Chuck." She took swift steps out of the kitchen. "I'm getting my gun."

Lauren didn't leave. Didn't move. She stood there. Unable to move.

What was the use of taking all of those lessons at the shooting range when she didn't keep her gun near her?

What use was it if she stood here like a frozen ice sculpture?

The cat wailed. A shrill sound that sent chills up Lauren's spine as she stared at a chubby young woman heading into the kitchen. Her were eyes wild, her brown hair dirty and scraggly. She wore boots, a worn-looking parka, and a pair of gloves. In her gloved hand, she held a knife. A hunting or fishing knife, shiny and sharp. It looked as if it could slice through an animal's skin and bones easily.

Humans were animals.

Lauren still didn't move. From the living room, she heard Chuck say, "What the fuck?"

The cat was jumping up and scratching the woman's gloved hand, but the woman ignored the cat, stepping closer to Lauren, her eyes unblinking. Sending terror through Lauren.

It was all happening fast. Too fast.

"You're ruining our lives," the woman said. "I have to stop you."

Before Lauren could think of something to say to her, the woman lunged toward her.

As she did, Falco lurched forward, clamping his teeth onto the woman's brown parka.

The parka ripped, leaving Falco with a mouthful of nylon, and the woman slowed and teetered.

Footsteps were running toward the kitchen, and Adam shouted, "Tori, stay back! Stay, Tori!"

The footsteps didn't stop.

The woman straightened, catching herself, turning toward Lauren again.

Lauren shuddered, her body unfreezing even

as she heard Sylvia running down the hall, toward the kitchen again. And Adam shouted louder, desperation in this tone, "Tori, go back to the living room! Go back!"

A thousand thoughts whipped through Lauren's mind, and one was prominent.

She needed to stop this woman.

She couldn't let anyone else get hurt because of her.

Before Lauren could move, the woman leaped into the air, the knife in her hand pointed at Lauren.

Then a black streak came from the kitchen counter, the small cat flying in the air, straight toward the woman. With a squawk, the cat lifted its right front paw, then slashed it down the left side of the woman's face.

The woman screamed and lost her balance, tumbling downward, slamming onto the wooden floor in front of Lauren, the knife popping out of her grasp.

Her breaths panting, the woman scrambled to her feet, shoved her hand in her jacket pocket and pulled something out. A gun.

"Get back, Lauren!" Adam yelled, rushing into the kitchen.

"I've got a gun," Sylvia shouted, running behind him. "Get away from her."

"I've got a gun, too!" Chuck called out.

Everyone seemed to have a gun but Lauren. There had to be a knife for cutting the turkey. She stepped back against the table, her hands behind her, and she felt the roasting pan that the turkey had been inside.

No knife. Damn it. The knife was on the counter. Her job had just been to spoon the stuffing out of the turkey and take it out of the pan. She hadn't needed a knife for that.

The crazy woman shifted toward the voices, dismissing Lauren as a threat. She raised her hand that was holding the gun, and pointed the barrel straight at Adam's head.

A silent *Noooooooo!* screamed in Lauren's head. She snapped around, grabbed the cast iron roasting pan, then swung it forward, smashing it on the side of the woman's head.

The woman screamed. Her arms flailed. The gun went off, sharp and loud.

Falco yelped.

The woman brought her arm up again. Falco clamped his teeth around the her arm, and Lauren turned the roasting pan upside-down and slammed it down hard on top of the woman's head.

The woman tumbled to the ground, falling onto her belly. Lauren didn't know if she had knocked her attacker down or if she had slipped on grease dripping from the pan. To be safe, Lauren dropped to her knees on the woman's back.

An outraged screech came from beneath her, and Lauren shoved the roasting pan back over the woman's head, the thick pan muffling her screams.

She looked up at the others. Adam was running toward her, Sylvia and Chuck behind him, both holding guns. Chuck's normally pleasant expression was grim. And Tori was peeking into the kitchen, her eyes big, Josh standing protectively at her side. Nate stood in the kitchen doorway, watching with interest.

For a moment, there was stunned silence, then another muffled scream came from beneath the roasting pan.

"Shut up," Lauren said, her voice low. Her breath gasping, she put her knee higher on the woman's back, at the top of her spine, and pushed down even harder on the pan.

The woman screamed. Never had Lauren been so happy to have a bony knee as now.

Immediately, Adam rushed to her, Chuck behind him. Everyone talked at once, and she sat back, finally letting go of the roasting pan.

"I'll watch her." Chuck pointed his gun at the woman. "This isn't the roasting pan, but it will kill her."

Lauren didn't reply. She looked at Adam as he helped her to her feet and then hugged her. She put her arms around him, her muscles weak and so was her hold on him. A freezing wind was coming from the back door, and she thought that not only was the woman on the floor a would-be murderer, she was also an energy waster.

"You're so brave," Adam said.

"I'm not ready to die," she said, her voice shaky. Not now. Not when he held her as if he never wanted to let her go.

And she held him tighter.

"I'll close the back door," Sylvia said, and as her footsteps started toward Lauren and Adam, faster and heavier thumping steps came from the open door, accompanied by heavy breathing.

"Piper!" a familiar man's voice cried. "Piper, don't kill her!"

Lauren stared, Adam's right arm still around her back, as Darryl, the insurance agent, puffed across the room, his face red and his breaths harsh. She turned to Adam and said, "We should call an ambulance."

"I already called the sheriff," Sylvia said.

"No need for an ambulance." Nate nodded at the woman at the floor. "I think she's going to be all right."

"Maybe she's not hurt, but I think Falco is." Tori knelt down at Falco's side.

Only then did Lauren realize that Falco was on the floor just a foot away from her. On his side was a streak of something that looked like grease.

Red grease.

Her mind rejected that. She hadn't spilled any grease on Falco. Besides, the turkey droppings weren't red, they were brown. Which meant it wasn't grease, it was...

A cry came out of her mouth. She jerked out of Adam's arms and dropped to her knees next to Falco, on the other side from Tori. Falco lifted his head toward her, and he whimpered.

"Falco! Oh, God, he's bleeding." She looked up at Adam, and he was on the phone.

"I'm calling the vet."

"It's Christmas!" Tears rolled down her cheeks. "What vet will take care of him on Christmas?"

Behind her, Darryl was saying, "Why, Piper? I told you not to do this."

"We had to do this." Her voice was high-pitched, and there were shuffling sounds as she got up to her feet. "I couldn't let you go to jail. What would happen to Mom and me? Who would take care of us?"

Anger flashed through Lauren. She shook with anger. She couldn't remember being this angry in...ever.

She still shook as she bent to kiss Falco and whisper that she loved him. She still shook as she got to her feet. She still shook as she turned to Darryl and the young woman who must be his sister.

"My dog." She kept her voice down only because if she raised it, Falco would be upset. "You shot my dog."

The woman shrugged. "It got in my way."

"You... You...*bitch.*" Without thought, she brought back her arm, then slammed her first forward and socked the woman's jaw, hearing the smash of fist against bone.

Her knuckles hurt like hell. She put her left hand over them. "Ow, ow, ow, ow, ow."

Adam pulled her to his chest. She hung on to him with one arm. She bent the other to her mouth to suck on her sore knuckles. She couldn't remember ever hitting anyone like that.

Behind her, Darryl's sister said, "She hit me! She hit me!"

"Shut up," Sylvia said, "or I'll have to shoot you. And believe me, everyone in the house will say it's self-defense."

"My brother won't."

"Your brother is apparently a criminal. So shut up or die."

The woman whimpered, but Lauren no longer

paid attention, looking into Adam's beautiful eyes. "I love you. But I need to take care of Falco now."

"I love you, too. While you were socking her"— he nodded at Darryl's sister—"I talked to the vet, and we can take him in right way."

She stared at him. Her mind felt numb. "It's Christmas. How did you—"

"I plow the vet's driveway at her home and the parking lot for her animal hospital."

"You're wonderful!" Tears welled in her eyes as she hugged him.

"The way to your heart is through your dog."

She pulled back to see him smile at her, but this time, she held back from hugging him again. And she held back from saying that he already had her heart.

"You have to stay here," Sylvia said, her tone matter-of-fact. "The deputies will want to talk to you."

"Falco is more important to me than the deputies," Lauren said.

"I'll take care of Falco." Adam knelt behind Falco. "I'll make sure he's okay."

Sylvia put her hand on Lauren's shoulder. "He's right. You need to be here."

Lauren stepped back. Sylvia was right, but it felt like the longest step she'd taken.

Adam turned down Chuck's offer to help, then he picked up her giant-sized dog. He only grunted once on his way up.

Her heart felt as if it were melting. In that second, she didn't care who else was listening. "You're my hero. You're my love." The emotion was overwhelming, and tears warmed her eyes. "I'll be single again soon. When I am, will you marry me?"

He grinned. "Ask me again when I'm not holding your dog with a bullet in his side."

Forty-five

Humans think with their bottoms instead of their tops. ~Pooka

Wow! Tori had to stop herself from clapping her hands together and squealing as her dad carried Falco out of the house. Lauren was biting her lower lip, her eyebrows contracted. Tori knew she was worried about Falco. But even with her worry, even though this weirdo woman had tried to kill Lauren, Lauren's face looked different. Soft and gooey. Tori had never seen her like that.

She was in love.

With Tori's dad.

Only Tori's concern about Falco kept her from jumping up and down and laughing wildly.

If there was one person in the world she would want to be her new mom, it was Lauren. Lauren had loved her mother, and her mother had loved Lauren.

It was almost as if her mom were up in the sky, pushing Lauren and Tori's dad together.

Tori didn't know if that were true, but if you

had to be wonderful to get to heaven, then her mom was in heaven.

Her mom would want her dad to be happy.

She would want Tori to be happy, too. Tori knew that.

And she would want Lauren to be happy. So it all made sense.

Josh was walking out with her dad to help hold the door open. Chuck was scowling, though he usually never frowned. It looked to Tori like he wanted to go with her dad, but he stayed in the kitchen to watch the weirdo sister and her pathetic brother, even though Sylvia was pointing her gun at them. And from the cool expression on Sylvia's face, it looked to Tori as if she wouldn't have any problem pulling the trigger.

The chubby woman was talking now. Whining to her loser brother that Lauren had knocked the roasting pan on her head.

She was even whining that her hair was greasy.

That was just more than Tori could take.

Josh walked inside as she took a step toward the brother and sister.

"Are you for real? You tried to kill Lauren. You shot her dog. You probably blew up her house, too. And now you're complaining about your hair? I hope when you're in jail, cockroaches crawl into your hair. I hope they crawl all over your face."

The woman started bawling. The brother just looked sad.

The guys started chuckling—Josh and Chuck. But the guy laughing the hardest was Sylvia's boyfriend.

Lauren put her arm around Tori's shoulder. As she drew Tori into the living room, Tori got in one last sentence to Lauren's attacker. "I hope all sorts of insects crawl over you."

The woman screeched. Once they reached the living room, Lauren bent to hug her. Not just a regular hug but an *I love you and don't want to let you* go hug.

Tori hugged her back just as tightly, and she wanted to cry. Not out of anger or fear but out of gratitude. Out of love.

It wasn't over yet. It wasn't perfect. Falco was shot, and she hoped he would be okay. She wanted him to be okay. He'd been so brave.

There was always something. She still had her diabetes, but she was young and took care of herself. And maybe there would be a cure soon.

In the meantime, Lauren would get her divorce and marry Tori's dad, and just the thought made Tori want to dance.

The wail of a siren came from down the street, and she and Lauren separated.

"Show time," Chuck said.

Lauren turned to him. "No, it's the time of reckoning."

Forty-six

Violence leaves a stain on the heart.
~Pooka

Home. Adam was home now. It had been a long day, and he'd spent an hour and a half in the vet's waiting room because a black lab had eaten turkey bones that were stuck in her throat, and a cat had blood in her urine. In the waiting room, the worried pet owners wanted to hear Adam's story, though he told them he didn't know anything.

It didn't matter. They wanted details, dragging out the basics from him, because refusing to say anything to his grandmother's cousin was impossible, and at least if he was talking, Susie Walters—who was a year older than him, and he and the other guys used to ogle her because she had developed breasts before the other girls—only stopped crying about her black lab when he talked.

So the trip to the vet hadn't turned out to be the slam dunk he'd thought it would be.

The good news was that Dr. Julie had said that Falco would be okay. She was only keeping him overnight because she'd sedated him before she'd dug out the bullet.

And when he came home to his house, Tori and Josh were there, waiting for him.

And so was Lauren.

The nightmare was over. Not over for good, because they were going to hear about it on the news, and they were probably going to be questioned again, and would probably have to testify at the trial later. But for now, he was in his warm house, eating leftover turkey and stuffing and even a cold bean salad with cashews and a slice of apple pie and a couple cookies with icing.

He ate like he was starved. He finally stopped eating, because he looked at his daughter, who was quivering with pent-up emotion. Her teenage heart *needed* to talk. It was a good thing he'd eaten quickly, because if he'd taken a minute longer, she looked as if she would surely burst from nerves and excitement.

And next to her was Josh. When Tori and Lauren were getting food for him, Josh had said he was going soon. He'd just been waiting for Adam to come home "in case other crazy people would try to attack Lauren and Tori." He'd stood. "But I'm going now."

How the hell could Adam let Josh go to the house next door with no lights and no warmth? On Christmas Eve, too? He'd told Josh that he should stay downstairs on the pullout couch. Just in case.

Josh had frowned, probably knowing it was

bullshit, and Adam had put his hand on his shoulder and looked him in the eyes. "We want you to stay."

Josh had bitten his lower lip and nodded slowly. And in that second, Adam had known they'd added an unofficial member to their family.

Adam sat back now. "I don't think I can eat another thing."

Tori made a sound like *eep*, then clapped her hands. "Then we can talk?"

"I'll put the food away." He started to get up, slowly, because he could feel the turkey torpor effect.

Lauren got to her feet faster than he did and pushed him down into his chair. "I'll clear. You sit. You're my hero."

"And you're my heroine."

"I didn't save anything."

"You saved the turkey and the stuffing."

Tori screamed and then laughed. Josh grinned. Lauren socked Adam's shoulder, and he reached for her hand, but she pulled away. "Dishes first."

"I hope you two aren't going to be mushy all the time." Tori giggled and jumped up. "I'll help."

She radiated happiness, and Adam followed Lauren's orders and sat back, too tired to argue. And too happy himself.

It was over. Falco would be back with them tomorrow. Back *here*. In his home.

They would be a family.

"After the table is cleared," Lauren said, "we have to talk."

Forty-seven

Everyone loves a happy ending.
~Pooka

The kitchen was clean, the dishwasher humming. Lauren could see the mental groan on both Adam's and Josh's faces as they sat in the living room. Lauren sat on the couch next to Adam. The kids on the stuffed chairs. Adam held a beer while Josh was drinking Christmas tea because that's what Tori was drinking, and Lauren guessed he didn't want to make Tori feel deprived by drinking hot chocolate in front of her.

Still, he was watching Lauren with the same wary look in his eyes as Adam. Lauren wasn't an expert on men, but she suspected that most of them dreaded the words were, *We have to talk.*

She crossed her legs. "Any questions?"

"On why they did it?" Tori looked at her dad. "The deputies made me and Josh stay in the living room while they talked in the kitchen. But we could hear everything."

Lauren took a gulp of her wine. She'd thought

Tori and Josh had been quiet in the living room. Too quiet.

"The brother's been stealing from the insurance agency." Josh turned to Adam. "As soon as you left, even before the deputies came, he was whining with excuses."

"Yeah," Tori said. "Their mom's obese and can hardly walk. She only wants to eat, and she can't work. He's supporting her and his sister. And food's not cheap, you know."

Lauren frowned. There was so much wrong with this.

"They have no money," Josh continued. "The sister has to be with her mom almost all the time, so she can't work, either. And now that Lauren's going to divorce her missing husband, they're afraid she'll sell the agency."

"Because *he* can't afford to buy it." Tori rolled her eyes. "Not after spending all the money on his mom and sister."

"And they're afraid someone will find out that the brother's been stealing," Josh said.

"Yeah," Tori said. "So she decided to kill Lauren, because then her brother can say that Lauren took the money, not him."

"And then they won't have to change anything," Josh said. "And that doesn't make sense, because then the first wife and her son will just sell it. No matter what they did, someone would find out."

Adam set down his beer on the coffee table. "People who are scared enough to kill aren't thinking straight."

Tori made a face. "The sister said she was

worried about her mom. But that's not love. Real love doesn't make you try to blow people up. Real love should've made her mom go to social services. Or her brother could've gone."

"That's what her brother said he wanted to do," Josh said, "but their mom refused to let them."

She glared at Josh. "They should've done it anyway."

"Yeah, but they were raised to hide their dirty secrets." Josh's expression darkened. "A lot of people are hiding dirty secrets."

"I bet she was embarrassed by her mom," Tori said. "I bet she really hates her."

Josh turned his head away.

In that second, Lauren wanted to go to him and hug him. But that would be the worst thing she could do.

"I think it's all of that," she said. "Embarrassment. Conditioning. And maybe anger. All of it spurred Darryl's sister to the breaking point, but that's not it, either."

"What is it?" Tori's voice was plaintive. "Can't you just tell us?"

"Fear."

There was silence. As if that word was taboo. They all looked at her.

And she knew that in many ways, she'd lived her life in fear. The reason she'd married a man she didn't love. The reason she'd taken so long to divorce him.

She'd feared that no one would love her. No one except her dog. So she'd settled for less than what she wanted.

Now she knew better. That fear might come

back, but right now she was filled with so much love that there was no room for fear.

"What now?" Tori asked.

"We all had a long day," Adam said. "Now we go to bed."

"I'll go to my bed." Tori raised her eyebrows at him. "But if Josh is sleeping in the basement, where's Lauren going to sleep?"

Lauren looked at Adam. "I'll go back to Sylvia's."

He reached over and took her hand in his. "Lauren is sleeping with me from now on. Isn't that right?"

Tears spurted in her eyes, and at the same time, she smiled so widely she felt her cheeks pouching out. "Yes." Her voice sounded hoarse. "From now on."

"You know what I want to do?" Adam said in a low voice, just for the two of them.

"I can guess." She smiled at him, because she was happy. And nothing could make her happier.

"Make babies with you."

Tears filled Lauren's eyes. She hadn't thought she could be any happier. But *this*... Then he was kissing her and she was kissing him back. She heard Tori's happy giggle and Josh's chuckle.

Adam pulled away from her lips, but only a couple of inches. "Merry Christmas," he murmured, for her ears only. "By the way, I love you."

As they kissed again, she heard Noelle's voice murmur in her head, saying directly to her, *"Happy Christmas, Lauren. And a happy life."*

Forty-eight

Love never leaves.
~Pooka

The small black cat was curled up on Tori's bed. "Pooka?" Tori asked.

Pooka opened one icy blue eye, then closed it. Tori quickly changed into fleece pajamas, then she went to the bathroom next to brush her teeth and get ready for bed. In her bedroom again, she left the light on and sat on the bed, her legs crossed.

"I'm not ready to go to sleep," she said. "Not until I know more."

Pooka opened both eyes. "What do you want to know?"

"Are you leaving soon?"

"Yesss. I'll leave after the sun is up."

"Did my mom send you?"

The cat didn't reply for a moment. "Maybe."

Tori nodded. She knew what *maybe* meant. It meant *yes*.

"Will you see her again?"

There was another pause, then Pooka said, "Maybe."

"Will you tell my mom I love her? And I'll always love her?"

"She knows. She feels the same way."

"I love you, too, Pooka." She blinked back tears as she uncrossed her legs and crawled under the covers. Pooka curled up to her side.

Tori closed her eyes. It had been the best Christmas ever.

Dear Reader,

Though bad things happened in this book, from the beginning to the end, this book was all about love in so many ways. As I wrote the book, I felt the love. I hope you did, too.

Thank you for choosing my book to read. If you would like to leave a review for this book, I would appreciate it. Your reviews help spread the word about an author's books.

The hero of book 4 will be Chuck, Sylvia's son. This series has everything I enjoy writing about— mystery, suspense, small towns, dogs, cats, and, above all, love. I plan to write many more books in this series. To find up when they're available, sign up to my new release email list at www.edieramer.com.

Because I love my own pets so much, I'm making Wednesday at my blog, "PET DAY." And not my pets. The pets of my newsletter subscribers. I'd love to hear about your pets and why they're special. I love pictures, too! You can contact me at my website at edieramer.com/contact/.

Happy reading!
~ *Edie Ramer*

Acknowledgments

Two main characters in this book have four legs instead of two. I live in Wisconsin. Before I wrote this series, I'd been to Door County a handful of times. But last April, to refresh my memory, I drove there with a friend, Kathryn Schowalter, and her Irish wolfhound, Cullen. Kathryn is witty and smart and fun. And Cullen was such a dignified yet friendly and gentle dog. (I was going to write *gentleman*, but then I reminded myself that he's a dog.)

Everyone we met smiled at us and many stopped to talk to us. As wonderful as Kathryn and I are—and as friendly as the Door County residents are—I'm sure that most of this came because of Cullen. I knew then that I would put him in a future book.

The second acknowledgment is for my gray cat, Belle. She probably weighs in about five pounds, but she thinks she's the boss of me. I think she is, too. She was my inspiration for my book CATTITUDE, and she also inspired the pooka.

About the Author

A *USA Today* bestselling author, **Edie Ramer** is funnier on the page than in real life. She writes stories with heart, attitude, and suspense. She lives in Wisconsin with her husband and one very important cat. She's happy to be able to do what she loves nearly every day. And she loves hearing from readers.